Mayer caught his breath for the first time since the cave. "What in the holy hell was that?" he said to no one in particular.

It was then that something hit the car from the side, strong enough to force Mayer off the road. As the occupants crashed into each other, Mayer quickly recovered and brought the Hornet back in line. Just in time for another hit to the side.

"What is that?" Cassi yelled out.

"The skinwalker," the shaman said matter-of-factly.

"You failed to mention it could outrun a car," Mayer said, just as a loud thud came from above them, then a scraping sound.

"It's on the roof," the shaman said.

"Ya think?" said Mayer.

The Hornet began to shake side-to-side, making it very difficult for Mayer to hold the road. The car's rear end fishtailed repeatedly, and at one point they were on only two wheels.

"He's trying to flip us over," Mayer said. He knew he couldn't keep the car on the road at this pace, and it was clear the skinwalker wasn't going anywhere. He thought for a moment, made a quick decision, then took action. As Mayer rolled down the window, he said to Cassi, "Take the wheel."

NIGHT MAYER

Legend of the Skinwalker
A Paranormal Noir

by

Paul W. Papa

NIGHT MAYER

Legend of the Skinwalker

Published in the United States by:
HPD Publishing
PO Box 230093
Las Vegas, NV 89105

ISBN (pbk): 978-1-953482-02-0; (10-digit) 1-953482-02-3
ISBN (ebk): 978-1-953482-03-7; (10-digit) 1-953482-03-1

Library of Congress Control Number: 2021909762

Cover design by Elizabeth Mackay Graphic Design
Edited by Melissa Parsons

Printed in the United States of America

HPD Publishing and the HPD logo are trademarks of STACGroup llc.

Keep up with Paul W. Papa's books at: https://paulwpapa.com/

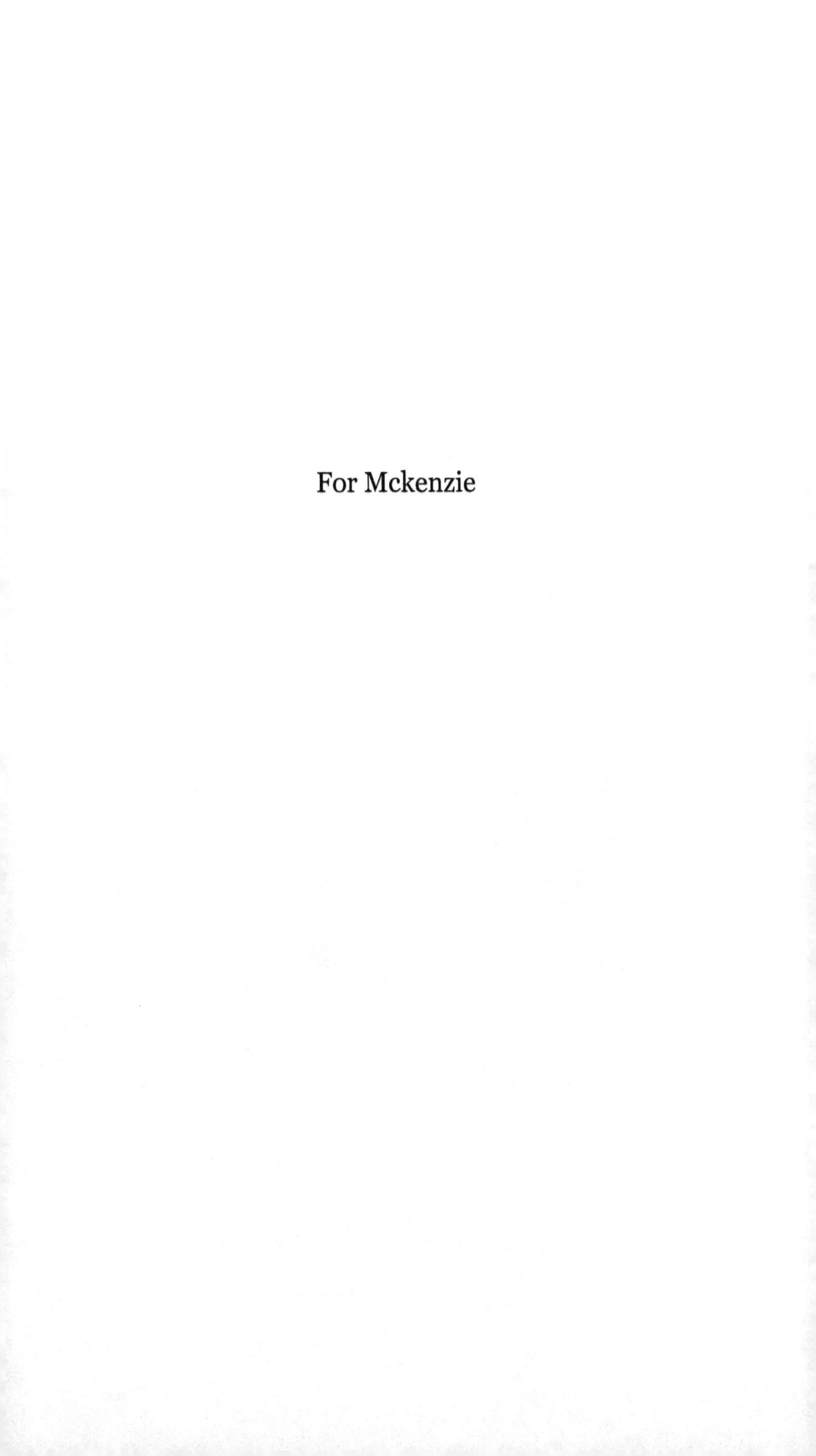

For Mckenzie

NIGHT MAYER

Legend of the Skinwalker

PRELUDE

A SHADOW CREPT steadily across the desk, covering the blueprints and obscuring the notes R. J. Hawthorne was making. "What are you doing here?" he asked with a bit of a huff. He wasn't expecting visitors, nor did he care to have any. He stopped making notes, but didn't look up. "You must have an appointment. You can make one tomorrow. I do not see anyone after hours. Now please leave."

The shadow did not move.

It had been one thing after another since they announced the project. Protesters, mostly from the local tribe of Paiutes, doing everything they could to block the resort development that he and his partner, William James Pierce, had started. It was prime real estate 25 miles outside of Las Vegas in the foothills of the Spring Mountain Escarpment. A place where water was plentiful and the temperature much cooler than its desert neighbor to the east.

The partners had a vision. People coming from all over to vacation at the base of the picturesque mountains, bathed in rich reds, blues, browns, and oranges. A modern dude ranch, complete with horseback riding, herds of cattle, and nights by the campfire. Of course, this dude ranch also had a pool, a spa, and a blue-ribbon chef. Some people would come to Las Vegas to gamble. Others to escape the drudgery of their daily lives. Still others would need something a bit more lasting—a permanent escape from the ones they once loved. Nevada's liberal divorce laws would make that possible.

He waited, not wanting to look up for fear that if he did, it would encourage the person to engage him in conversation. It was late and all he wanted was to finish his notes on the revisions, then head for a good meal and an even better nightcap. But the shadow stood its ground. He laid his pencil purposely on his desk and let out a second huff. It was clear this person was not going to leave unless he addressed him specifically. "What do you want?" he asked and looked up.

He was met with an inexplicable sight. At first he thought it was a Paiute dressed in some kind of ceremonial garb. It happened quite often. The protests turning into makeshift powwows with dancing and drums beating incessantly. But this was no Paiute. In fact, he wasn't even sure the thing in front of him was a man at all.

Though it stood on two feet, those feet were nothing human. Thick hair cascaded downward from just below the knees to the claws protruding from beastlike toes. The hands, like the feet, were covered in thick, brownish-gray fur. Fingers, ending in sharp claws, were held at the ready. The beast loomed over him. Its head had the shape of a wolf . . . no, a coyote, grotesquely blended with that of a human—pointed ears and saliva dripping from yellow-stained fangs.

Hawthorne shoved his chair back hard and scrambled for the revolver he kept in the bottom drawer of his desk. With a trembling hand, he took hold of the .38 and pointed it at the beast. The creature made a guttural growl, but did not move.

"I'm not afraid to use this thing," he said, as firm as he could muster.

The creature took a step closer, then another.

He pulled the trigger. The echo bounced off the walls in the small office. He'd hit the creature in the chest, but it had no effect. He fired again and again, but nothing happened; nothing stopped it from drawing closer. Its yellow, bewitching eyes—more human than creature—bored into him.

Several seconds passed before he realized the gun was clicking with each pull of the trigger. The creature glared at him, meeting his eyes with its own. He wanted to look away, but he couldn't. Something compelled him, controlled him. The creature took one final step, only inches away from him now, its furious breath defiling his cheek. The putrid stench filled his nostrils and worked its way into his lungs.

He dropped the gun.

It was the eyes. They captured him, peered inside him. Deep inside. Piercing and then stripping away a hidden veil. Though the creature was still in front of him, something had changed. Something dreadful. It was now inside of him as well. It overtook his mind and controlled his limbs.

He sat back down in his chair. picked up the revolver, and laid it on his desk. Then he calmly opened the top drawer and took out a piece of blank paper. He wrote the date at the top, then wrote more. Much more. When he finished, he positioned the paper at the corner of the desk. Then he picked up the revolver, opened the cylinder, and emptied the shells. They bounced from his desk and fell to the floor. He filled the weapon with six new bullets, fresh from the same drawer where he had gotten the .38. He brought the gun to his head—his eyes wide and his mouth agape.

If anyone had been around, they would have heard the echo cascading throughout the canyons and would have come running. But there was no one to hear. No one at all. So the sound faded into the mountains and vanished.

1

"YOU READY FOR the show?" Joe Sobchik asked as he handed his friend P. M. Mayer a highball glass filled with ice and rum.

Joe was an easygoing gent. Clean-shaven with kind eyes, a bright smile, and a hairdo that might have been a pompadour if he had put more time into it. He wore a white shirt, the top button open, the sleeves doubled over, like the cuffs on his pleated trousers.

"You mean the spectacle, don't you?" Mayer retorted. He took the offering and settled into one of the two lawn chairs Joe had set aside on the roof in anticipation of the event, positioning his cheaters against the sun.

Joe lit a Lucky and took the blue lawn chair next to Mayer, beer in hand. "Call it what you will," he said. "It's good for business."

"Shouldn't you be working?" Mayer asked.

Joe leaned back in the lawn chair. "Even working stiffs deserve a break."

Mayer sipped his rum and scanned the crowd. The typical collection of misfits: dancers, performers, musicians, and a guy who'd made it big when his low-budget film caught fire in the theaters at the beginning of the year. Every one of them with a drink in hand. It was early in the morning and most of those in attendance were still working on the previous day.

Mayer was just another one of those misfits who'd gathered on the roof of Atomic Liquors for an unobstructed view—suit coat slung over the back of his lawn chair, tie undone, lid tilted toward the front—waiting for the ghastly show of human ascendancy. Just as bad as the rest of the blokes.

He usually enjoyed the stillness of the new morning, washing over the town, cleansing it of all its sins. Bringing with it the hope of a better day, before it was once again sullied by the stain of night.

But this morning had none of that feeling. None of that hope. The stillness, instead of refreshing, seemed somehow stale. People stood, like mannequins in a store window, facing west on Fremont Street, their eyes pinned to the sky. Children had been brought in buses to a nearby baseball field where bleachers provided a better view. The sun had not yet peeked above the horizon to scorch the day. Yellow clouds, looking more like fire than hope, blanketed the area. The neon marquee atop the Hotel Apache was still shining bright, and Vic was still greeting guests at the New Pioneer Club with a hardy "howdy pardner" from his position high above the fray. Just as if it was a regular day. Just as if nothing dreadful were about to happen.

"You've got to give this town credit," Joe said. "When faced with, well, lemons, they made margaritas and turned it into a party."

"Only in Vegas," Mayer added and lifted his glass in salute.

Joe was right, of course. When a trucker on his way to town saw a strange mushroom-shaped cloud and reported it to the local paper, instead of trying to fight the testing of nuclear weapons, Las Vegas transformed it into a business opportunity.

It didn't take many brains to discover what was going on. The scientists at the test site made it easy. They stayed in the Last Frontier and every single one of them requested 2 a.m. wake-up calls. They boarded the same plane at Nellis Air Force Base and flew out to the test site at the same time. Even a politician could figure out what was going on. But the biggest clue came in the form of a bright light resulting from the blast. Hard to hide something that could be seen as far away as San Francisco and Los Angeles.

Las Vegas took to atomic testing like a lizard to a hot rock. They set up a point, called News Nob, on Spring Mountain where invited media could watch the spectacle from afar. The Chamber of Commerce produced a calendar of scheduled blasts, hotels organized viewing picnics, bakeries created mushroom cloud cupcakes, and restaurants added things like atomic burgers to their menus. Hairdressers created atomic hairdos and Las Vegas High School put a mushroom cloud on the cover of their yearbook, the Wildcat Echo. Copa Girl and blonde-haired beauty, Lee Merlin, was even crowned Miss Atomic Bomb.

American capitalism at its best.

Joe did his part, of course. He offered viewing parties, created an atomic cocktail, and even named the bar Atomic Liquors.

A female called to Joe from the opening to the roof. Mayer recognized the voice, as did his companion. It was Joe's wife and co-manager, Stella. "No rest for the wicked," Joe said and climbed out of his chair. He turned to Mayer. "I'll be back," then added, "maybe."

Joe had no sooner left when Mayer was approached by another. "Excuse me," a female voice said, her soft, flowery perfume lighted the stale air. "Aren't you the one they call 'Night Mayer?'"

He pulled off his cheaters, tilted his lid, and rubbed his eyes. The sun seemed brighter in the morning than at any other time of the day, though he knew that wasn't really the case. "Depends on who's askin'."

"Name's Cassi Reyes," she said. "Pleased to meet you."

She likely extended her hand, but Mayer didn't look up to find out. He replaced his cheaters, pulled his lid down over his eyes, leaned back in his chair, and took another drink. He knew who she was. Cassi Reyes. Hank Greenspun's newest cub reporter, hungry for a story, trying to make a name for herself on the pages of the *Las Vegas Morning Sun*. She had telephoned him several times seeking an interview. He never dialed her back.

She stepped in front of his chair, blocking the sun, stencil pad and pencil in hand. "You're a hard man to get ahold of."

"Moonlight Mist," Mayer said.

"Excuse me?"

"Your perfume. It's Moonlight Mist by Gourielli."

"How did you?" She let the question fall. "I'd like to ask you about the Sloan Canyon incident."

He took another sip and ignored her.

"Awful early to be drinking, isn't it?" she asked.

He lifted his cheaters and took a close look at the woman. The sun from behind her created an eerie aura that framed her slender figure. She wore high-waisted brown slacks that gripped tight to her legs above the ankles, a thick belt of matching color holding them in place. The collar on her white, long-sleeve, button-down blouse was kept high, and she had on flats that matched her slacks. Her own tortoiseshell cheaters rested atop her head, blending into her short pixie-cut brown hair that was awash in highlights, or maybe the sun was hitting her just right. He wasn't sure.

"Who let you up here?" Mayer asked and replaced his cheaters. "This is a private party."

"One of the owners, thank you," she said smartly.

"Frank?"

"Who's Frank?" she asked. "Joe Sobchik let me in."

Mayer made a mental note to speak to Joe about the impropriety. "I don't do interviews," he said.

It didn't stop her. "Why do they call you Night Mayer?" she asked.

"Lack of imagination," he stated blankly.

"I'm afraid you've lost me."

"My name's P. M. Mayer," he said. "P. M.—night, get it?"

"Clever," she admitted.

"Hardly," he said, then added, "Look, if you're here to see the show, then grab a chair and a drink and relax. Otherwise, scram."

The newshawk did little to hide her disdain. She flipped the cover of her notebook so hard that she dropped the newspaper she was holding. Mayer bent over, picked it up, and was about to hand it back to her when the headline caught his attention.

LOCAL DEVELOPER COMMITS SUICIDE

"What's this?" he asked.

"R. J. Hawthorne killed himself last night."

"Why would he do that?"

"How should I know?" Cassi said and extended her hand. "Can I have my paper, please?"

It was just at that moment that a blast of light lit the morning sky. The woman dropped her cheaters over her eyes and turned toward the light. Several seconds later, as the force of the shock wave swept through the town, the ground shook and the crowd on the roof took a collective breath, then cheered as the distant cloud began to form in the morning sky. Mayer watched as the unnatural thing climbed higher and higher into the heavens, displaying its malevolent might—the abominable glory of the human race. And as it did, in a town replete with the possessed, fiendish, and soulless, Mayer wondered what a blast like that might unleash on an unsuspecting town.

2

MAYER STOOD IN front of the mirror, feeling much older than his thirty-two years, washing his rough, stubble-filled face in the sink of Atomic Liquor's restroom. He could probably use a shave, but Mayer wasn't the kind of man who shaved regularly. In fact, it had been the better part of a week since he'd last done the chore. Shaving was for real men, with real lives, who held down real jobs. Not for people who went about skulking in the night. Not for him.

His eyes were blue this morning. They had been green yesterday, though his driver's license claimed they were hazel. Mostly they were bloodshot. But today they matched the color of his tie. He'd picked up the tie at a secondhand store, the same place he found his suit and the trench coat he often wore. He didn't really need the extra layer in a town like Vegas, but he saw Bogie wear one in a movie once and liked the look. Not today though. Today it would be too hot, even for him. He replaced his lid and suit coat, but didn't bother tightening his tie. What good would it do?

Stella was tending bar when Mayer emerged from the bathroom. The spectacle had ended and most everyone had long since left. Including the nosy brunette. He took a seat at the bar.

"You gonna make it?" Stella asked.

"Jury's still out," Mayer said. Stella poured a club soda and slid it across the bar to him. "Who let in the newshawk?" he asked.

"She lied to Joe," Stella said. "Said she was here to do a story on our rooftop view."

Mayer had known Stella nearly all his life. Their mothers had been the best of friends and were very close. Stella's mother, Waleryia Virginia Zasucha, came to Las Vegas in 1921 with Stella and her older sister, Helen, in tow. Virginia started as a cook for the Union Pacific Railroad and eventually became a caregiver for Judge John Busteed. When he died, Busteed left Virginia the property on Fremont Street between Ninth and Tenth. She turned it into a service station and eventually a diner called Virginia's Café. Stella and her husband Joe took over when the diner was running on all eights, eventually changing the place into a liquor store and tavern, branding it Atomic Liquors.

Mayer went to Las Vegas High School with Stella and Helen, the eighth class to graduate from the high school Las Vegas built on the outskirts of town in 1931. The Union Pacific Railroad had donated the property to the town, and George A. Ferris & Son designed the building in the Art Deco, Aztec Moderne style. Their mothers' friendship led to one of their own, one that became even more important to Mayer after his parents disappeared.

"Where is Joe?" Mayer asked.

"Oh, he's out on the roof," she said, then added. "Don't be too hard on him."

He didn't plan to be. Joe, too, was an orphan—a kindred spirit. He and Stella were the only family Mayer had, or wanted. Reporters tricked people. It was what they did.

"You got the paper?" he asked.

"Looking for a job?" she kidded as she slid it over to him.

He gave her half a smile, then unfolded the thing to the front page headline and began reading.

LOCAL DEVELOPER COMMITS SUICIDE

Developer Richard Jones Hawthorne was found dead in his office, the victim of an apparent self-inflicted gunshot wound. Hawthorne and his partner, William James Pierce, were slated to build a resort-style dude ranch in the Spring Mountain Escarpment, complete with horses, cattle, and campfires, though some claimed the resort was simply a way station where men and women could stay long enough to establish residency and get the divorce they so sought.

The project has met with resistance from the very beginning, from both the local Paiute Tribe, who claims the land as a sacred burial ground, and from Vera Krupp, owner of the neighboring Diamond V Ranch. Krupp had met Hawthorne and Pierce in court, on several occasions, trying to put a stop to the resort. A temporary injunction was granted for a study of the impact on the area, and the project was currently on hold at the time of Hawthorne's untimely death. The fate of the site is uncertain as Pierce was unavailable for comment.

"Ain't that a bite?" Mayer said to no one in particular.

"Whatcha got there?" Stella asked from behind the bar. She had the same sparkling eyes and dark brown hair as her mother. And while only five foot tall on a good day, she'd kept Joe and Mayer in line on more than one occasion. She was a woman unafraid of getting her hands dirty. Mayer liked that about her.

"Some developer shot himself out there by Diamond V Ranch," Mayer said.

"Why'd he do that?"

"Who knows? Probably got himself in financial difficulties, or ran afoul of the trouble boys. Either way, it didn't end well for him."

A deliveryman stepped into the bar, his muscular arms pressed into a clean, light blue, button-down shirt, his name embroidered on a patch over the pocket. The cuffs on his dungarees were rolled up and he was wearing work boots, the laces tied around the top. He had a coif of blonde hair done up in a proper pompadour and no lid. Mayer reasoned he was likely the favorite of the local ladies—the strong, silent type.

"Got a delivery," he announced.

"Pull around the back and I'll open the door for you." Stella told the deliveryman. She turned to Mayer. "Watch the bar for me?"

Mayer nodded. He placed his lid on the bar, then took off his suit coat, folded it, and laid it on the stool. He slipped behind the bar, rolled up his sleeves, and began washing glasses. Mayer tended bar when he needed a buck or two—which was more often than not. Stella tried to get him to work it full-time—the customers liked his drinks, she told him—but some people weren't meant for steady jobs.

Mayer had been behind the bar about twenty minutes when a gentleman who definitely had the bees strolled in the side door. He wore a dark brown, double-breasted sack suit, with a matching waistcoat, vest, and double-pleated trousers, full in the hips and tight at the ankle. His tie matched the tip of the display handkerchief resting in his top pocket and his shoes were Jarman—at least they looked like they were. He fit in about as well as an olive on an ice-cream sundae. He took a measure of the place, then sat down at the bar.

"What can I get you?" Mayer asked.

He eyed the colored bottles resting on the shelves in front of the large mirror behind Mayer, probably searching for something he thought he could keep down. "Macallan," he said finally. "On the rocks."

Mayer laughed. "Macallan?" he repeated. "Does this look like a place that would have that kind of hooch?"

The man removed his brownstone Stetson Ambassador and laid it gingerly on the bar. "What brand of," he paused, "hooch, does an establishment such as this serve?"

"How 'bout some Old Fitzgerald?" Mayer offered.

"Very well," the man said.

Mayer removed a glass from the shelf behind him, taking extra care to make sure it was clean. The man seemed like the type that would prefer a clean glass. The cross from the rosary beads wrapped around Mayer's right wrist clinked against the glass as he filled it with ice, then poured the scotch inside. He laid a small square napkin on the bar and rested the drink on top.

The man took a tentative sip. "Smooth," he exclaimed, but his face betrayed him.

Mayer poured himself a cup of Joe and brought it to the bar. "You seem a little out of place," he said, then added, "Not that you aren't welcome here."

The man looked at Mayer intently, eyeing first the rosary beads, then the onyx bracelets on his left wrist, ending with the strange tattoo on his forearm. "Might you be the man they call Night Mayer?" he asked.

It was a popular question.

"Who's askin'?"

The man stuck out his hand. "Name's Pierce. William James Pierce."

Mayer took the offering. "What are you doing here, Mr. Pierce? And what do you want with me?"

"I have a job offer."

"I'm afraid you have the wrong man," Mayer said. "I don't know anything about resorts, dude ranches, or quickie divorces."

Pierce smiled. "That is not why I'm here," he said. "I was told you had a hand in the Sloan Canyon incident. I was hoping you could do the same for me."

"Not interested," Mayer said.

"Perhaps this will change your mind." He reached into his suit coat and pulled out a long slim wallet. Alligator skin. He opened the thing, pulled out a crisp one hundred dollar bill, and laid it on the bar.

"You'll have to do . . ."

Before Mayer could finish, Pierce laid down four more bills just like it.

"That's a lot of cabbage," Mayer said.

"I'm told you're worth it," Pierce countered.

"Who told you that?"

Pierce waved him off and tried another sip with the same result. Mayer watched with interest as the man removed a fancy silver cigarette case from his other inside pocket, took out a single slim, brown cigarette, and offered one to Mayer. When Mayer declined, Pierce closed the case and slipped it back where it came from. Then he placed the thing between his lips and lit the end.

"Why do you need me?" Mayer asked. "The hammer and saws have this one all figured out. You think they've missed something?"

"Richard Jones Hawthorne was not the type of man to commit suicide."

Mayer laughed again. "If there's one thing I've learned in life, mister, it's that no man knows what another man will or won't do."

"That may very well be true," Pierce said, "but I know my partner, and even if he did commit suicide, he'd never leave his share of the resort to Vera Krupp." He said the name as if it was bitter in his mouth. "Now, do you accept my offer? I'm not a man who enjoys wasting time."

Vera Krupp? Mayer thought. That information wasn't in the newspaper. And Pierce had a point. Why would a man leave his share to a woman who had tried to thwart him every step of the way, then shoot himself?

"Perhaps I was wrong," Pierce said and began lifting the bills from the bar, one at a time. Mayer watched as he tapped them together to align the edges and opened his wallet. He slid the bills inside and returned the alligator skin to his inside pocket. "I'm sorry to have wasted your time," he said. "What do I owe you for the drink?"

Mayer studied the man. There was a weary concern in his eyes. And while he was dressed to the nines, those same eyes told Mayer that Pierce hadn't seen sleep in quite some time.

"Let's not be hasty," Mayer said. "Tell me more."

3

AN HOUR LATER, Mayer was sitting at the desk of Homicide Detective Raymond C. Fry thumbing through a file marked "PRIVATE" in bold, block letters. The detective bureau was crammed into a small space on the third floor of the Las Vegas Police Department. An odd array of worn-out, wooden desks pressed together edge to edge filled the room, and the only man who had his own area was the Lieutenant, a man named Connor McQueeney, according to the name painted on the door.

"Open-and-shut case," Fry said. "The goose clipped himself."

Fry was the consummate dick. He drank too much, smoked more than he should, and knew more about human behavior than anyone in the department. Lessons learned from years as a bull, working the rails. He joined the force when the Union Pacific Railroad pulled out its service and repair yards over a labor dispute and had been there ever since, working his way up to detective. He probably should have been running the place, but as he'd repeatedly told Mayer, he didn't want the headache.

Fry looked like a flatfoot more than any man should. He was tall and thick, with a square jaw and deep-set eyes. The sleeves of his white shirt were rolled up to his elbows—his tie loose around his neck. He wore gray flannel trousers, his matching suit coat and Stacy Adams resting on a coat rack behind him.

Mayer worked with Fry on the Sloan Canyon incident and the two had established a working relationship that, if they weren't careful, could border on friendship. Mayer understood Fry. But more importantly, he trusted the man. Fry had done Mayer a favor and pulled the file from the Clark County Sheriff's Department, who had jurisdiction over the unincorporated area where the resort was to be placed and the incident occurred.

Mayer read the report. Hawthorne was found slumped over on his desk by his partner William James Pierce. He had a single shot through the temple, the bullet cutting a clean path through his brain. The five other bullets remained in the .38, unfired. There were no signs of a break-in or a struggle, and nothing was missing. The note Hawthorne left was also in the folder.

I, Richard Jones Hawthorne, do leave my share of the Spring Mountain Dude Ranch and Spa to Vera Krupp to do with it as she pleases. This is my final wish and I make it of my own free will and accord. I hereby commit my soul into God's hands.

Fry leaned back in his wooden swivel chair—the arms black with wear. "The boys at the lab did a bang-up job on this one. The only prints on the piece were his, and he had gunshot residue on his right hand. Suicide. Plain and simple."

Mayer was skeptical. He lifted the paper. The dated and signed note was flat and void of folds—the ink clearly indenting the paper. The writing was smooth and even, as if it came from someone who wasn't rushed.

"And you don't find it strange that he left his share of the project to a woman who'd been fighting him in court?"

"Of course, it's strange," Fry said, "but men do strange things and the science don't lie. Besides, it's not my case. The brown boys can handle it just fine." He leaned forward. "Say, why are you so interested in this anyway?"

"His partner came to me today. Doesn't see Hawthorne as the type to pull his own trigger."

"Well, my in-laws still don't understand how my wife married me, but she did."

"They aren't the only ones wondering," Mayer said.

"Ahhh," Fry exclaimed and waved him off.

Mayer examined the folder further. Fry was right, there was nothing to make it look like anything other than a suicide. Even the coroner listed the cause of death as such.

"That coroner report came back awful quick," Mayer noted.

"Hawthorne's an important man," Fry said. "Important men get to move to the head of the line, even in death."

"And the ME?"

Fry shook his head. "No need for an autopsy," he said. "Coroner ruled it a suicide."

Mayer was about to close the file when something caught his eye. In the list of evidence removed from the scene were seven empty shell casings from a .38 revolver. The same .38 Hawthorne used to send himself to the afterlife. "Who shoots their heater six times, empties it, fills it with six more, then turns it on his own head?" he asked.

"Richard Jones Hawthorne," Fry said, matter-of-factly. "I already told you, the science don't lie, kid. So what if it took him six times before he screwed up enough courage to put the thing against his own skull? No sin in that."

Mayer wasn't convinced.

"Maybe he was playing knucklebones and ran low on jacks." Fry smiled at his own humor.

Mayer did not.

"Go tell your sugar daddy there ain't nuttin here," Fry said as he pulled a smoke from the pack on his desk and lit it. A regular man would have been offended, but Mayer understood Fry didn't mean it as a jab against him. It was meant for Pierce.

"He's barking up the wrong tree," Fry said and blew out a puff of smoke. "Tell him that instead of wasting his time, maybe he should make nice with Vera Krupp if he wants to keep the project moving forward. Though I doubt it would do any good."

Mayer stood. He handed Fry the file and thanked him for the favor.

"Keep your nose clean, kid," Fry told him.

Mayer climbed into his midnight blue Hudson Hornet and headed back down Fremont Street to Atomic Liquors. He'd told Pierce to meet him back there in a couple of hours and would tell the man if he'd take the job or not. Pierce was sitting at the bar when he arrived.

"I presume you went to the police department," Pierce said.

"You presume correctly," Mayer confirmed. He laid his lid on the bar next to Pierce.

"And?"

"And the coroner lists it as a suicide," Mayer said. "Hawthorne's are the only prints on the weapon, and there's gunshot residue on his right hand. Looks like your man killed himself."

"So you agree with the police?"

"Sheriff," Mayer corrected, adding, "and, I didn't say that." There was something about the report that troubled him, something that didn't quite fit. Though he couldn't put his finger on just what that was. "Just because a man offs himself, doesn't mean he committed suicide," Mayer said. "I need a look at the crime scene."

Pierce stood. "We can take my car."

4

MAYER OPTED TO take his own car, following Pierce to the site. He wasn't sure where the day would take him, and he didn't want to be beholden to another man's ride. The drive out to the Spring Mountain Escarpment was long and boring, filled with nothing but brown dirt, cacti, sagebrush, and visible waves of heat. He rolled down his windows, but the air outside seemed even hotter than the air in his car. Mayer's Hornet didn't have air conditioning, not like those fancy new Bel Airs. Even if the option was available, he wouldn't have been able to afford it. His bankroll was more day-to-day than long-term. As he drove, Mayer wondered what possessed William and his brother J. Ross Clark to build a town in this godforsaken place—the Devil's vacation home. No coincidence that its closest neighbor was called Death Valley.

Every so often Mayer passed a stray burro who would gaze at the intruder with the same disdain a stranger received when walking into a saloon for the first time. He wondered what the animal made of the big, blue car as it sped by.

They headed down Blue Diamond Road toward the small town of the same name. Both the town and the road got their moniker from the Blue Diamond Corporation, which built the place to house most of its 325 employees who worked its gypsum mine atop Blue Diamond Hill. It was an ugly hill, void of vegetation. Having nothing to claim as beauty, except for the curvy semi-horizontal striations that ran along its side.

They turned right on the dirt road that led to the mine, passed both the small town and the hill where the mine was located, then kept going. The scenery made a remarkable improvement in this area. The escarpment rose skyward, out of the desert, toward the heavens on Mayer's left. Majestic, jagged mountains of brown, green, orange, and blue, seeming to come out of nowhere. A horizontal patch of deep red striped the mountains, looking very much like a child darted alongside them, holding out a paintbrush as it ran. The sight made even the desert below more appealing.

A couple more miles down the road and the Coupe deVille Pierce was driving turned left onto another dirt road—this one heading directly toward the escarpment. As Mayer bounced down the corduroy road, his lid flew off, landing onto the seat next to him. He quickly rolled up his window in defense of the dust that seemed intent on filling his car. The dirt road led to a white, rectangular, ten-wide trailer coach. Wires connected the thing to a large pole some twenty feet away. This, Mayer presumed, must be the office.

The yellow caution tape was still in place when they arrived, and a brown boy, as Fry called them, from the sheriff's department was standing guard. Another man stood next to him. He wore a black suit, heavy on the black. His slacks and fedora the same shade of darkness. Wayfarers protected his eyes from the sun—or maybe it was the other way around. There was a slight bulge below his left arm and another at the bottom of his right leg. A hatchet man.

They weren't the only ones there. Newshawks surrounded the place like ants at a picnic, likely waiting for Pierce. Mayer pulled in next to the man's car. When Pierce stepped out of his Cadillac, not a hair was out of place. His car, Mayer figured, must have air conditioning. Pierce slid his lid onto his head and was immediately surrounded. The hired gun came and helped him wade through the crowd as reporters shouted their questions.

"Why did your partner commit suicide?" one yelled out.

"Will you still build?" asked another.

"Is it true Hawthorne left his part of the project to Vera Krupp?"

The question stopped Pierce in his tracks. Mayer guessed that nugget of information hadn't yet been released to the public and wondered how this particular newshawk discovered it. He looked at the reporter, smiled, and moved on. It was Cassi Reyes, and when she didn't get an answer from Pierce, she moved to Mayer.

"What are you doing here?" she asked as Mayer stepped out of his Hornet, closed the door, and replaced his own lid.

"I'm hoping for a quickie divorce," he said and kept walking.

Trailer coaches were rolling rectangles, with painted aluminum panels, resting on tractor-trailer frames. They were becoming very popular as places to live. A home on wheels. Mayer wondered what they'd think of next. This particular one was set in place on some type of support system covered by lattice panels. An iron flight of stairs allowed entry.

Mayer followed Pierce up the stairs and inside. "How'd you get this thing down that road?" he asked.

"It was easier than you might think," Pierce said. "We had a very large truck."

"Must have been a doozy."

The hired gun opened the door for them, then waited outside.

From the moment Mayer stepped inside the trailer, he felt it. The heaviness of death. It filled the place, overpowering the room and sitting still in the air. It was accompanied by an unearthly stench, and flies, hundreds of flies. Enough to make a pie—if one were so inclined. Pierce pulled out a monogrammed handkerchief to cover his nose and mouth. Mayer didn't bother.

The trailer was set up like an office. Two desks rested on either side of an oval-shaped table that Mayer assumed was used for meetings. One desk—the one closest to the door—had a deep brown stain atop it, like melted chocolate, covering a set of blueprints. Mayer had seen it before. The color of dried blood. There was an impression of a head, or what was left of one. That seemed to be a favorite resting spot for the flies.

"This where you found him?"

"Yes," Pierce said, handkerchief in place. He pointed. "In that chair, his head on the desk."

"The door, was it locked when you arrived?"

"No," Pierce said. "I told R. J. to keep the door locked when he was here alone, but he didn't listen."

Mayer walked behind the desk, being careful where he stepped. He looked down at the floor. Some of the blood had dripped down and pooled there. He wasn't surprised. Head injuries always had so much blood. He looked at the other desk, mere feet away. Gray brain matter was splattered all over it and along the wall.

Mayer hated brains. Grotesque looking things.

"What are you planning to do with this thing?" Mayer asked, referring to the trailer.

"Burn it," Pierce said. "After you prove Hawthorne was murdered."

"You might not want to wait."

Mayer opened the bottom drawer to the desk. He knew Hawthorne would have kept the gun there. People always seemed to keep guns there—in the bottom drawer. He didn't know why. If he had an office, Mayer's heater would be in the top drawer, easily within reach. He was rewarded for his effort with an open box of shells.

"Why did Hawthorne have a gun?"

"Coyotes," Pierce said quickly, then added, "And protesters who might get out of hand."

"You got one too?"

Pierce shook his head. "Don't need one," he said.

Mayer pointed to the door, referring to the man on the other side.

Pierce nodded.

Mayer took his handkerchief from his back pocket. He used it to pull the box of shells from the drawer. More than twelve were missing. "He fire his heater often?"

"Sure," Pierce admitted. "To scare off coyotes."

"That it?"

"That's it," Pierce said.

Mayer placed the shells back in the drawer.

"You two have a row?"

Pierce's face soured. "Of course not, why would you ask that?"

"Just covering all angles."

Mayer looked at the desk. According to the title block, the blueprints were of the proposed dude ranch. Various notes were scribbled in pencil on the top page. "Where was the note?" Mayer asked.

"There," Pierce said, pointing to the corner of the desk.

Mayer examined the area. It was clean. "No blood on it?"

Pierce shook his head.

Mayer studied Pierce. He looked like a man used to getting his way, one for whom things always seemed to work out in his favor. He wondered why Pierce hadn't just destroyed the note when he found it. It would have been easier. Simpler. People don't always leave suicide notes. No one would have known. He decided to ask.

"Why didn't you destroy the note when you found it?"

Pierce looked at Mayer with displeasure, taking his time to answer. "What kind of man do you take me for, Mr. Mayer?"

"A man who wasn't alone, I'm guessing."

"My man was with me," he admitted.

"Just your man?" Mayer asked.

Pierce nodded. It wasn't a convincing nod, and Mayer didn't buy it.

"And why do you think this is my area of expertise?" Mayer asked.

"I don't know that it is," Pierce admitted. "All I know is that R. J. Hawthorne did not commit suicide and even if he did, he would never have left his part of the business to that kraut. Things happen at times. Things that can't be explained. I'm told you're the one people turn to when that occurs."

It was something Mayer had come to accept. His town was indeed a hotspot for ghosts, goblins, and the like. In Vegas, everything bumped in the night. And why wouldn't it? A city based on the most sinful needs of men couldn't help but attract the corrupt, the depraved, and the degenerate, all leaving their smudge on the town. It's why his parents moved here. The possibility for research was endless.

Mayer looked at the man hard. "If you want me to look into this, you're going to have to be square with me." He paused. "On the whole crop."

Mayer waited while Pierce reviewed his options.

"Then you find my terms acceptable?" he finally asked.

"To a point," Mayer said. "That much cabbage will buy a lot, but not everything and not forever."

"All I need for you is to look into this. If you have additional expenses, you may submit them to me. As for other things, I have a man for that."

"I imagine you do," Mayer said.

Pierce returned his handkerchief to his pocket, then opened his wallet and removed the five bills he'd laid on the counter at Atomic Liquors. He offered them to Mayer, but Mayer didn't take them. Instead, he just waited for Pierce's answer.

Pierce let out a sigh. "R. J. hired a housekeeper," he said. "She was here with us."

"Before you got here?"

"No, she arrived when we did. We all walked in at the same time."

"Still doesn't explain why you didn't just destroy the note. Tip your mitt, Pierce, or I walk."

"She also works for Vera Krupp."

Mayer did his best to hold in a laugh. "Well ain't that a bite?" he said. But it was clear to him now. Pierce needn't explain any further. The maid had seen the note. More importantly, she had seen what was written on it and if Pierce tried to destroy it, all it would do is create far more suspicion. Better to look for foul play, no matter how hard that road might prove to be.

Mayer took the bills and slid them into the pocket of his suit coat, then he continued giving the place the ups and downs. But there wasn't anything there. Nothing at all. Nothing to suggest a man didn't simply commit suicide. So why couldn't he rid himself of the feeling there was something here—something that didn't meet the eye?

"You usually get here first?" Mayer asked.

"Yes, R. J. typically comes in toward the early afternoon. That is, if he doesn't sleep here."

Mayer raised an eyebrow. "He do that often?"

"Often enough," Pierce said shortly.

Mayer walked behind the desk and stood there for a moment, letting the environment engulf him. Trying to understand what would entice a man to stop making notes on a blueprint, pull out a gun, and send his tormented soul to the great beyond. Even more so, what would make a man fire six shots before he did the deed?

Mayer looked down at the floor. Six shots. Six empty shells found on the floor; having fallen after being ejected from the gun's cylinder. He turned back to the question he'd had when he spoke to Fry. *Who shoots six times*, he wondered, *then fills the gun anew with six more bullets?* And then it hit him.

Mayer looked up at the wall directly across from him. The wall of an aluminum trailer. He stared at it so hard that Pierce, handkerchief back in place, turned to look as well.

"What are you looking at?" Pierce asked.

"A wall," Mayer answered. "A wall with no holes in it."

5

"I DON'T UNDERSTAND," Pierce said.

Mayer examined the other walls and found no holes in any of them. He looked up at the ceiling. It was the same. "This trailer is made of aluminum," he explained. "Not the strongest of metals. Nothing that would stop a stray pill from traveling right through to the outside. If someone sat here and pumped six shots before reloading, why aren't there any holes?"

Pierce turned to the wall. It was clearly a question he hadn't considered. It was a question the sheriff's deputies must not have considered either—or they didn't care.

"Was Hawthorne in the habit of keeping his old shells?" Mayer asked.

"Not that I'm aware of," Pierce said, then added, "But I have to admit, I didn't keep track of his weapon. Dirty things, guns."

Unless someone else is holding them, Mayer thought. He stepped outside and took a deep breath. Pierce followed, removing his handkerchief when he hit the fresh air. The newshawks were still lined up. Pierce's hired man and the deputy kept them at bay. Mayer walked to the rear of his Hornet and opened the trunk. Inside, artfully arranged, was an array of items that, had Mayer ever been pulled over by the authorities and had his trunk searched, would've been difficult to explain. Bottles of holy water, cases of bullets, some cast in silver, cartons of salt, knives with silver blades, aerosol cans, pistols of many different calibers, an iron club, flashlights, rope, a machete, and two shotguns. He also had multiple crosses—some made of silver, some iron—a Polaroid camera, and film.

He pulled out the camera, checked for film, and headed back inside. He stopped at the stairs when something on the ground caught his eye. Hoofprints. Horse hoofprints, to be exact. At least they looked like horse to him. Though, Mayer figured, they could have just as easily been burro.

Once he got inside, Mayer took pictures of everything in the room. What was there and what should have been there, but wasn't. He stopped when he noticed hairs on the floor, bent down and picked them up.

"You got a dog?" he asked.

"Certainly not," Pierce said through his handkerchief.

Mayer examined the hairs. They looked like dog to him, but what did he know? Brownish-gray, with just a touch of white. Mayer pulled out his handkerchief and placed the hairs inside, before folding the thing and sliding it back into his pocket.

"How many people entered this place this morning?"

"I would have no idea," Pierce admitted. "There were the three of us and a myriad of police."

"Sheriff's deputies," Mayer corrected. "I think we're done here," he said. "I'll keep you informed."

"We don't have much time," Pierce said. He reached in his pocket with his free hand and gave Mayer another of his cards. "Courts tend to act quickly in these matters."

"See if you can stall them," Mayer suggested. He was about to leave when he noticed a piece of Hermes luggage against the wall near the corner of the room. Horsehair canvas protected by Bordeaux leather around the edges and at all corners. Certainly not a coffee and donut piece.

"That yours?" Mayer asked.

Pierce shook his head.

"Hawthorne in the habit of keeping clothes here?" Mayer asked.

Pierce nodded. "He liked to hike the area," he said through his handkerchief. "He kept a change of clothes and work boots."

Mayer took the suitcase by its leather handle and lifted it onto the conference table. He popped the two latches and had a peek. Inside were clothes a man might indeed use for hiking. A long-sleeve button-down shirt with flaps over the pockets—Western style—and twist twill slacks accompanied a covert-cloth jacket. There was a pair of thick socks and dark brown engineer boots.

He packed everything back the way he'd found it, like his mother had taught him, closed the latches and rested the Hermes back on the floor. Everything inside the suitcase seemed right, but it was the outside of the thing which bothered him. *Why*, Mayer wondered, *would a man as well off as Hawthorne not put his initials on an expensive piece of luggage?*

After he returned the camera to his trunk, Mayer had a look around. Below the towering red sandstone peaks, the desert was awash with all manner of vegetation, each battling for a cherished spot in the landscape. A dark green Spanish bayonet poked out between two large, multicolored sandstone rocks that seemed to have been thrown by some angry god, landing haphazardly in the sand. The area abounded in blackbrush, cheesebush, and ephedra, also known as Mormon tea, on account of the Mormons who settled there in the 1800s dried and boiled its leaves, using it as both medicine and beverage.

The desert, while colorful in places, was a harsh mistress. It played with heat, inviting one in with warm comfort, then stealing away the breath. The majesty of the mountains hid the dangers that lurked below. Plants, like the spiny menodora, concealed long needle-like spines behind inviting white flowers. Cholla cacti, not quite as deceitful in their appearance, were spread throughout the area, reminding people of the dangers associated with venturing too far off any given trail—not that there were many to take. None of it, however, seemed to bother the thousands of burros, horses, and coyotes that make the place their home. Not to mention the birds, rabbits, lizards, snakes, and spiders.

Yet the desert had its own beauty, if one but looked. Purple mountains, like the ones in the famed song, bleeding into deep reds and bright pastels. Cacti that at certain times of the year displayed the most beautiful flowers and edible fruit between their prickly thorns.

Pierce and Hawthorne had chosen one such place. It was about as far away from the sins of Las Vegas as one could come and was also much cooler—by ten to fifteen degrees at times. In Mayer's opinion, it was a good choice, though the thought of disturbing the natural landscape saddened him. While the place was secluded, it offered visions as far as one cared to look. And in one of those places was a dark horse, on top of which sat a rider in a white Western-style shirt, sporting an equally white cowboy hat. The horse and rider were both pointed in Mayer's direction.

"Who's that?" Mayer asked.

Pierce looked to the horizon. "That'd be Vera Krupp," he said.

"She always this interested in the goings-on around here?"

"At times."

"I'll be in touch," Mayer said, then got into his car.

He headed back up the pitted road, this time choosing to leave his lid on the seat next to him. When he got to the end, in relatively one piece, he turned left and headed farther along the original road. About a mile up, he found another entrance to another dirt road on his left. A sign indicated the entrance to the Diamond V Ranch. Mayer took it.

The road was in better condition than the one leading to the trailer, but not by much. A little ways down, Mayer was forced to stop and wait for a train of burros to cross. They seemed to be on their own time schedule and were unaffected by his horn. *Perhaps*, Mayer thought, *they knew something he didn't.*

The road eventually led to a sturdy ranch house resting upon a knoll that spread out to the right into a sloping acre of honest-to-goodness green grass—an oddity in the desert. Just to the left of the house was another spacious field that, instead of grass, was filled with cattle. Mayer had no idea it was a working ranch, nor did he know cattle could be raised in Southern Nevada. But if grass could be grown here, why not cows? He parked his Hornet on the side of the road, donned his cheaters and lid, and got out, then took the manicured trail leading up to the house.

It was an expansive place with rustic sandstone walls and a wooden shake-style roof. The front door opened to a covered porch that extended out at an angle from the eaves. Two large, mullioned windows on the left side of the door completed the facade. A structure to the right side of the house looked much like a barn, and was likely an add-on to the original at some point, its deep-red siding a fitting augment to the sandstone.

Mayer was about to make his way to the rear of the house when he was approached by an elderly man with a broad nose and round leathery face that had been dried and tanned in the desert sun one too many times. He was clothed in dungarees and a well-worn Western-style shirt. His eyes were covered by cheaters, a furry caterpillar had taken residence on his upper lip, and his gray hair, which had likely once been black, was tied in braids and laid across either shoulder. Mayer guessed he was Paiute, but it wasn't much of a guess as the Southern Paiute was the local tribe. He was perfectly in place here, right up to the wide-brimmed hat atop his head.

"Can I help you?" the man asked.

"Possibly," Mayer said. "I was hoping to speak with Vera Krupp."

"Mrs. Krupp is not available right now. She's . . ."

"May I help you?" another voice came from behind. It belonged to a dusty blonde dish in calf-length pants and a light blue gingham blouse. Horn-rimmed glasses rested on her petite nose and a scarf was wrapped smartly around her neck. She held a stenographer's pad tight against her chest.

"I'll take it from here, Buster," she said. "You may go."

The man nodded and left.

"How may I help you, Mister . . .?" She let the word trail off.

"Mayer. P. M. Mayer. I was hoping to speak with Vera Krupp. I'm guessing you are not her."

The woman stood her ground, acting as a slender, but sturdy wall between Mayer and the house. She was polite, but firm. "I'm Peg Westburg, Mrs. Krupp's personal secretary. What is this in regard to, Mr. Mayer?"

"Oh, I think you know the answer to that question."

"Mrs. Krupp has already spoken to the authorities. She has said all she has to say. You may please leave."

"And what about her housekeeper?"

"Excuse me?"

"Her housekeeper. The one that Hawthorne and Pierce also use. Has she said all she has to say?"

If Peg Westburg was flustered by the comment, she didn't show it. "I'm sure she has as well," she said.

"So the sheriff's deputies spoke with her?"

"Perhaps you should take that up with the sheriff, Mr. Mayer."

But before Mayer could answer, a tall horse supporting a brown-haired, hazel-eyed rider clopped around from the back of the house.

6

"TAKE WHAT UP with the sheriff?" the woman on the horse asked. She was dressed in the same white Western-style shirt and hat Mayer had seen earlier. Only now he could see her features. They were round and smooth, with pillow cheeks and a feminine chin. Her lips were the exact shape lips ought to be and her hazel eyes kind. Movie star looks. Fitting, because that's what Vera Krupp once was—a movie star, in Germany anyway. And while that life was now many years in her past, she still seemed to carry the spark that had, at one time, made her a starlet.

"Vera Krupp?" Mayer asked.

"I explained to Mr. Mayer that you were unavailable," her secretary offered, probably wanting to show she was, indeed, fulfilling her duties as gatekeeper.

"It's all right," Vera said with a light German accent as she slipped easily from the saddle. Her mount was a tall chestnut stallion with dark socks and a distinct white patch on its muzzle, a measure of rope looped over the saddle's horn.

Vera was much smaller off the horse, but still a respectable height. Somewhere around five foot five, Mayer guessed, a woman who shined as much in her

Western garb as she did in glad rags and pearls. She flipped the reins over the saddle and glided over to Mayer. "Nice to meet you, Mr. Mayer," she said extending her hand. "How may I help you?"

Mayer took the offering. Her grip was surprisingly firm, not the delicate thing Mayer had expected. The hand was soft though calloused. This wasn't the grip of a movie star, but of a rancher, a woman who worked with her hands for a living. Mayer was impressed.

It was also the hand of a deputy sheriff, another thing Mayer hadn't expected. Pinned to her shirt over her left breast was a six-point gold star, each point softened by a small circle. The badge carried the imprint of the Boulder Dam, surrounding which were the words. "Vera Krupp Special Deputy Sheriff, Clark Co. Nevada." Accompanying the badge, a chrome-plated six-shooter with a pearl handle hung from a holster on her right hip, much too high to be of any use. It seemed to Mayer that the pistol was more for show than function. In fact, he wondered if it was even loaded. Krupp's current choice of duds also caught Mayer's attention. In his opinion, white hardly seemed the color one would wear on a working ranch. It made him wonder for whom the show was meant.

"I was hoping to speak with you about the unfortunate incident across the way there," Mayer said.

"If you mean the death of R. J. Hawthorne," Vera offered, "I wouldn't call it unfortunate."

"Then you don't find sorrow in his demise?"

"Should I?" Vera asked casually. She walked over to the fence and wrapped the reins around the top post. "Tell me, Mr. Mayer, do you ride?"

"Horses?" he asked.

"What else?" Vera countered.

Though he'd grown up in the West, Las Vegas specifically, Mayer had never been on a horse—that is, if you didn't count the coin-operated kind outside the Safeway on Second Street.

"Sure," he lied. "Why do you ask?"

Vera turned to her secretary. "Peg, have Buster bring Jasmine around the front. Mr. Mayer and I are going for a little ride."

"Yes, Mrs. Krupp."

Mayer thought about all the times he'd been warned of the consequences of straying from the truth. He was about to suffer one of those now.

"I'm not really dressed the part," Mayer said, holding his suit coat open.

"I guess you aren't at that," Vera said. "Perhaps another time." She unstrapped the reins and headed toward the house, her horse in tow. Peg walked with her.

He hadn't fooled her. But he did need to speak with her.

"I still have questions," Mayer said. "Like how your name got on a suicide note?"

That stopped Vera Krupp in her tracks. She handed the reins to her secretary and motioned for her to continue on ahead, then she turned to Mayer. "Walk with me," she said.

Mayer did as told.

"This is a working ranch, Mr. Mayer," Vera continued. "Did you know that?"

"I did not," Mayer admitted.

She opened the gate to a log fence and motioned for Mayer to enter. She chuckled when Mayer placed his hand out, preferring she go first. "We don't stand on ceremony here, Mr. Mayer."

Mayer nodded, then walked in. After he entered, Vera closed the gate behind them, hooking the wire loop over the top of a shorter post, making it impossible for animals void of opposable thumbs to free themselves.

"I purchased the ranch from Chester Lauck. I'm told he was a radio personality."

"He was," Mayer confirmed. "Lum and Abner, they were called. Ran the Jot 'em Down store on their show."

Vera gave a cursory smile and kept walking. "He leased it for four years from William George who had plans for a chinchilla farm. At least that's what I'm told. It was Mr. George who built the original home, the foreman's house Buster lives in, and the shed for his chinchillas. He also expanded the orchard. Mr. Lauck eventually purchased the ranch from Mr. George and named it Bar Nothing Ranch," she said, then added, "a name I quickly changed."

They walked across what passed for a pasture, but was really just the desert, heading for a herd of cattle. Vera kept up her history lesson.

"It was Mr. Lauck who added the sandstone building that is now my home."

"You and your husband, you mean."

Vera stopped and looked purposefully at Mayer. "No," she said. "I said it correctly."

"So your husband doesn't live here?"

It was an unnecessary jab, but Mayer took it all the same. Mayer knew quite a bit about Vera Krupp and her husband, Alfried Krupp von Bohlen und Halbach. He had become somewhat of an authority on all things German after his mother and father disappeared in Germany. Mayer's parents were both experts in the paranormal and the occult. Something the United States government found handy when they started battling Hitler—a man obsessed with the occult. It was that work which likely cost the pair their lives and Mayer his childhood.

Vera's husband was the son of Bertha Krupp, the heiress to the Krupp munitions dynasty. Alfried took over the business from his ailing father, Gustav Krupp von Bohlen und Halbach, shortly after the outbreak of the Second World War. In 1945, Hitler changed the inheritance law, essentially taking the business away from Alfried's mother and giving it to her son. Mayer didn't have a lot of rules, but one of them was definitely to never trust a man who double-crossed his own mother.

If providing a dictator bent on world domination with the weaponry to do so and double-crossing his own mother wasn't enough, Alfried took every opportunity to make as much money off the war as he could. He used concentration camp slave labor, seized property in every country Hitler conquered, and sent people to the gas chamber if they didn't play along. After the war, he was tried and convicted of war crimes at Nürnberg and sentenced to twelve years in prison, but it didn't stick.

The U.S. high commissioner, a man named John J. McCoy, granted Alfried amnesty in 1950 and restored all his holdings. The only caveat was that he isn't allowed on American soil. That restriction didn't hold for his wife.

Vera sat on the edge of a watering trough as several small brown calves with white heads and stomachs ran over to her, acting more like dogs than cattle. Her face lit up as they approached. "These are my calves," she said proudly, wrapping her arms around one of their necks. "I've crossed white-faced Herefords with Brahmas to create a breed more suited to the desert environment."

"Fascinating," Mayer said, just as the shadow of a bird crossed over him. It was a large shadow, much larger than any bird should be able to make. He resisted the temptation to duck, then looked up to the sky.

A hawk was circling. Mayer thought it a red-tailed hawk, but couldn't really tell. He remembered the bird from a field trip in Mr. Tyndall's biology class, how it floated on the air for hours at a time. It made him wonder what it would be like to be a hawk. With no real predators to speak of, the bird could catch the wind, like a surfer a wave, wings spread outward, lazily following the current as it pleased. Not a care in the world.

In reality, it was the only bird he remembered from the class, so every time he saw a creature soaring high above, floating on the air, its wings stretched wide, he simply assumed it was a red-tailed hawk. Who was going to correct him?

This particular hawk, assuming it was one, seemed to be especially interested in what was happening directly below—the very area where he and Vera currently stood. Its circles were tight and specific, and it was either looking at them, or honing in on prey. And just as it circled around yet again, Mayer swore he could see two bright red dots where the bird's eyes should be. He pulled his cheaters down and squinted in the sun, just as the bird turned and flew away.

"Let's not let's pretend, Mr. Mayer. Why don't you tell me why you're really here?"

Mayer turned his attention back to Vera, then tapped his own chest above his left suit pocket.

Vera looked down at her badge. "Oh that," she said. "Had some trouble here on the ranch one time. Takes too long for the sheriff to get here, so I asked Butch to deputize me. He obliged."

The Butch Vera spoke of was W. E. "Butch" Leypoldt, who took over the position of Sheriff from Glen Jones, the founder of the Sheriff's Posse, the Aero Squadron, and protector of the most famous sex factory in Las Vegas—Roxie's Resort. That was, until the FBI raided the place and Greenspun exposed Jones' connections to the establishment, causing him to lose the office he'd held for twelve years, coming in dead last of the five candidates that ran for sheriff that year.

"Your housekeeper," Mayer said, "she also worked for Hawthorne?"

Vera focused her hazel eyes on Mayer, taking an account of the man. "I'd bet you already know the answer to that question, Mr. Mayer, but since you seem to need a confirmation, yes, she did."

"For a man you didn't particularly care for? Even hated?"

"Hate is a very strong word, Mr. Mayer. I didn't hate R. J. Hawthorne. I just didn't care for the business he was in or his plans for the land."

"Yet it's perfectly all right for you to run a business here."

Vera grew stern. "This ranch has occupied this soil in one form or another since 1834, when it was a way station to those traveling along the Spanish Trail. We have not desecrated the land around us and have left the area mostly as it was originally. In fact, the buildings which made up that early campsite still exist to this day, more than a hundred years later. And as far as my housekeeper goes, who am I to deprive her of work? She must come out here anyway. It's convenient for both of us."

"I guess it is at that," Mayer added. "Do you mind if I speak with her?"

"I'm afraid she's not here today."

"When will she be here?"

"Tomorrow, but she's already spoken to the sheriff. I doubt she'll have anything different to tell you, Mr. Mayer."

"All the same. I'd like to try."

Vera stood. "You haven't asked the question you really came here for, have you?"

"I guess I haven't at that," Mayer admitted.

"Well, go ahead then."

"What would make a man who considered you an impediment to his progress, a man you met in court on more than one occasion, give you his share of the project just before committing suicide?"

"I'm sure I don't know."

"Awful convenient isn't it?"

"What is it you want to hear, Mr. Mayer? That Mr. Hawthorne and I had an illicit affair? That I allowed him into my boudoir so I could beguile him into signing over his portion and then rid myself of him by encouraging suicide? I assure you, Mr. Mayer, I am not eine Hexe?"

Mayer didn't answer.

"I have no more idea why the man named me on that note than I do why he would commit suicide in the first place."

She paused and a strange melancholy seemed to overtake her. She ran her fingers, absentmindedly, over the head and ears of the calf next to her. Mayer let her have the moment, wondering what the thought was and where it had taken her. After a bit, she came back and turned her attention to Mayer.

"Come back tomorrow, Mr. Mayer," she said, as she moved to the gate. "If Bessa agrees, then you may speak with her."

Mayer tipped his hat, thanked Vera, and took his cue to leave. As he made his way to his Hornet, he chanced one last glance up toward the sky. The hawk had returned.

7

WHEN MAYER GOT to the end of the dirt road, he pulled to the side, climbed out of his car, and glanced skyward. The hawk was still there, floating high above him. He thought for a moment that maybe it wasn't a hawk after all. Perhaps it was a vulture and Mayer was dead but didn't know it. Or maybe it was an eagle, or even an osprey. Though the birds weren't common, they did at times make the area their home, and any of the three would be larger than a hawk. And while that might account for the size of the thing, it didn't explain the glowing red eyes.

Mayer slipped back into his Hornet and pointed it toward town. When he got there, he headed north on highway 91, then took a right onto Fremont Street before heading to the coroner's office. He asked to see the body of R. J. Hawthorne and was led to the morgue by a twenty-something assistant in a long white coat. It was an antiseptic place full of freezer-style doors that open to compartments that housed the dead, laid out on metal slabs, tags clinging to toes. It was not a place unknown to Mayer.

The assistant opened the door to Hawthorne's little apartment and slid out the tray which bore his body.

"Crazy story this one," the assistant said.

"Oh? How's that?"

"Japser had the world by the tail. Then he goes and offs himself. For what?"

"You tell me?"

The assistant was taken aback. "How should I know?" he said. "If you ask me, it's probably some dame. It's always a dame."

"That what you think?"

"Sure. Why wouldn't it be?" he said with the conviction of a much older man.

"Could've been a bread shortage," Mayer offered.

"Naw, this bird had dough coming out his ears. My money's on a dame. Want to see him?"

"If you don't mind," Mayer said.

"Get ready," the assistant said. "This one'll creep you out."

He pulled the starch white sheet from Hawthorne's head, revealing a distorted face frozen in fear—his eyes wide and his mouth agape.

"Can you imagine?" the assistant asked. "Dyin' with your mug pasted like that?" he shivered visibly.

The assistant had a point. What would make a man bent on killing himself twist his face like that? He'd seen the aftereffects of several men, and some women, who'd offed themselves. But never once had he seen fear on their faces. Sadness, yes. Even a quiet resignation of their fate, but never fear. Not like this anyway. This was the face of a man seeing something he didn't want to see, experiencing something he didn't want to experience. Mayer was becoming more and more convinced that Pierce was right—Hawthorne didn't kill himself.

After the assistant slid the body back into its cubby, Mayer thanked the man, slipped him two bits, then headed back to his Hornet. He made his way onto San Francisco Street, took a left onto Talbot, then a right onto Canosa. He pulled into the driveway of the shotgun house four doors down on the right and got out of his car.

He threw on his lid, brushed the desert dust off his suit, and bounced up the stairs, but before he could ring the bell, the door opened. On the other side of the screen was Theodosia Petulengro, an olive-skinned Romanian with thick, brown eyebrows resting above inkwell eyes and prominent lashes. She was dressed in a patterned, flowing circle skirt and a peasant blouse with short, ruffly sleeves that was pulled dangerously low—enough to show off a pair of ample breasts. A gold strand laced around her neck. Her black hair was covered with a bright red scarf; gold beads and medallions dripped from the top and rested upon her forehead. A streak of white hair peeked out from the left side.

Theodosia was a fortune teller who dressed the part—mostly for her clients—and while much of what she did was for entertainment purposes, Mayer knew well the gift she brought out only on special occasions, and only with the right people.

"Hello, Theo," Mayer said.

"Hello Prometheus. Won't you come in?"

Theodosia was one of the few people in Mayer's world who knew his real first name and one of the even fewer who were allowed to use it. It was a handle given to him by his mother, Doris, a student of Greek mythology and paranormal studies. She received her three degrees at Berkley and it was there, working on her doctorate, that she met Mayer's father, Elias, whose family left Germany in 1914 when the Great War broke out. Doris Blaine-Mayer bestowed upon her child the Greek name of Prometheus, meaning forethought. And, as if that name wasn't difficult enough, she tacked on the middle name of Makarios, meaning blessed in the same language. Not easy names to have as a kid.

When she was still alive, Doris would drag her only son to Theodosia Petulengro's house where she routinely received tarot readings. The two women became fast friends when Doris recognized immediately Theodosia's true powers. His mother saw her as a confidant, and, because of that, so too did Mayer.

It was Theodosia who had given him the onyx bracelets he wore on his left wrist—just where she had told him to place them. The rosary beads came from a priest—one who, like Mayer, had seen far too much not to believe.

Instead of the front showroom parlor—decorated much like the inside of a gypsy caravan—where she entertained most of her guests, Theodosia took Mayer down the hallway to the kitchen in the back of the house. She offered him a seat, then turned to the stove where a kettle of hot water was at the ready.

"Earl Grey?" she asked.

Mayer nodded, placing his lid on the table.

She removed a porcelain cup from a peg under the cabinet. It had a gold brim and a pattern of red dog roses along one side. Steam, like the mushroom cloud this morning, rose high as Theodosia covered the leaves she'd encased in a silver infuser with the hot liquid. She placed the cup on a matching saucer and handed it to Mayer.

He let the leaves steep.

"You always did like it dark," she said, then smiled as she poured herself a cup and took a seat at the table across from him. "I was told you might be coming, but there was no indication as to why."

"I have another case," Mayer said. "One that should be open-and-shut, but doesn't feel that way."

"And what do you seek from me?"

"Understanding, as always."

"I can't promise you understanding," Theodosia said. "The tarot can only aid you on your journey to fulfillment. The cards reveal a possible pathway. A door you may or may not choose to open. Nothing else."

"Enlightenment then," Mayer said.

"Drink your tea," Theodosia said, then pulled out a deck of cards from a pocket under her skirt. They weren't the cards she used with her regular guests. No, these were a family heirloom, plainly decorated, passed down from mother to daughter for more generations than Mayer could recall. Of course, Theodosia knew them all and every morning, just after she rose, she thanked those who had come before her, those who had passed down the gift.

She handed the deck to Mayer, clasping his hands in hers, as she always did, briefly before letting the deck go. Her hands were soft and warm. The cards were tattered, but only around the edges—age, not abuse.

"Hold the cards and consider your question," she said as she lit the sandalwood candle resting on the table. "Bring yourself into the cards."

Mayer thought of what he wanted to ask, knowing that the question had to be worded properly. He knew silly things like *Should I have taken this case?* or *Is Pierce telling me the truth?* would be met with harsh criticism on the part of Theodosia, and the cards. If he wanted a proper answer—a proper reading—he first needed to understand the question.

He thought of everything that had happened already. Of Hawthorne and the will, the suicide, and the missing holes in the wall. He thought of the hairs he found on the floor, the housekeeper, Vera Krupp, and the hawk soaring high in the sky, following him, circling its prey.

Theodosia instructed him to shuffle the cards, making sure to keep them facedown. She didn't have to tell him that each time she read for him, but she did anyway. When the deck was shuffled, she gently took the cards from him and held them next to her chest, keeping her eyes closed. There was a stillness in the air, and the room seemed a bit colder than it had only a moment before. But it was nothing new to Mayer. Nothing he hadn't felt before.

He tried his tea.

Theodosia began dealing the cards into three stacks. This was known as the three-card spread. It was a common type of reading in that it allowed each of the positions to guide the seeker, as each represented an aspect of the question—past, present, and future. Each a part to consider.

"Ask the cards your question," Theodosia said.

"What forces will I be dealing with and what should I consider as I proceed?"

Theodosia flashed him an approving smile and motioned for Mayer to turn over the top card of the first stack. After he did, she placed it between them in the first position. The card showed the profile of a blindfolded woman in a white robe, holding a pair of crossed swords.

Theodosia laid the card just as Mayer had turned it, upside down—the reverse position.

"You are confused by your plight and are unable to see either the problem or the solution," Theodosia said.

"Story of my life," Mayer added and took another sip of tea.

"You seem to be missing information. Something that would make your decision clear. You must look harder. Use both your head and your heart to weigh the options," Theodosia said. "Take in the situation as a whole. Trust your intuition."

Theodosia motioned for Mayer to turn over the second card. The three of pentacles. On the face of this card was the image of a stonemason working with his tools. An architect on either side held the designs for the building, which was meant to represent a cathedral. The architects were bearded, elderly men, while the stonemason was young.

Theodosia chuckled as she placed the card down on the table, to the right of the first card. "In order to succeed, you must do something you do not enjoy," she said, then added, "work as a team."

"Dandy," Mayer said, but he'd meant to keep it in his head.

"There is value in different levels of experience," Theodosia said. "The stonemason cannot build the cathedral without the help of the architects. Neither can the architects build the cathedral without the stonemason. Each must play their part. The older architects respect the skill and knowledge of the stonemason, while the young stonemason appreciates the wisdom of the architects. Neither operates from a position of superiority.

"You must be willing to learn from others, Prometheus, understand that they too have something to offer, regardless of their background or level of experience. Once you have your plan in place, you must understand that each person on the team has a role to play and a unique contribution to make. This is not something you will be able to accomplish alone."

Mayer's day was getting better and better, which is why he shouldn't have been surprised at all when he turned over the third card. The one he hated to see the most.

8

"OH DEAR," THEODOSIA said as she placed the overturned card in the third position, reversed. "It seems the six of clubs has come back for yet another visit."

This deceitful little card hid behind the innocence of two children, a boy and a girl, the boy handing the girl a bouquet of flowers. Love, harmony, and cooperation. But not when in reverse.

"You continue to live in the past," Theodosia said, then she took his hands in hers. "You must let go of what happened to them. The cards are clear. You continue your private stroll down memory lane, holding onto the fear and the pain." Theodosia looked intently into

Mayer's eyes. "You must forgive yourself, Prometheus. What happened was not your fault."

Mayer pulled his hands back. "That's just it, isn't it? I don't know what happened. One day they were here and the next . . ."

He didn't finish the sentence.

"Your parents knew what they were getting into. They understood the risks."

Sure. They knew what they were getting into, chasing Hitler and his search for the occult halfway around the world, but what about Prometheus Makarios Mayer? How was a seventeen-year-old kid about to graduate high school supposed to deal with it all? How was he supposed to make something of himself without the influence of the two most important people in his life?

"You got something stronger than tea?" Mayer asked. "I could use a stiff hooker."

Theodosia stood and moved over to the cabinet. "I think I have some Carioca," she said. "Unless you'd rather have brandy?"

"No. The rum will do," Mayer said.

She poured a couple of fingers in a short glass and handed it to Mayer. It was sweet and smooth, just what Mayer needed to chase away the demons.

Theodosia took her seat. "Do you want to tell me about the case?"

"You sure you want to hear it?"

She nodded.

"You see the paper this morning?" he asked. "The article about R. J. Hawthorne kicking himself off?"

"I saw it," she admitted.

"Well his partner, William James Pierce, is convinced that good ol' R. J. could never have committed suicide, and he wants me to prove it."

"What do the police say?"

"Sheriff's department ruled it as a suicide. Open-and-shut case. His prints on the gun, burn marks on his hand, no sign of forced entry, nothing missing. No one to blame but Hawthorne."

"And where do you fit into all of this?"

Mayer tapped his nose. "Just what I asked Pierce," he said. "But he didn't have a good answer."

Mayer told Theodosia about the visit to the trailer, about the hairs he found on the floor, the hawk that seemed to follow him, and the red eyes.

"Hawks are guardians," Theodosia said. "They often carry messages from our ancestors. They are gatekeepers of the East, representing honesty and clear vision." She paused. "Did it's shadow pass over you by chance?"

"Did it?" Mayer exclaimed. "Not only did it pass over me, it almost overtook me."

Theodosia rubbed her hand gently across her lips.

"What is it?" Mayer asked.

"Hawks are warriors of truth," she said. "If a hawk passes his shadow over you, it means you are in danger."

"Ain't that a bite," Mayer said.

"You know that area behind the ranch is sacred to the Paiutes, right?"

"I know."

"What is your plan?"

"I'll have to go up there and have a look around, won't I?"

Theodosia stood. She walked over to the kitchen cabinet, pulled a piece of paper from a small notebook and a pencil from the carnival glass holder. She wrote something on the paper, brought it back to the table, and slid it over to Mayer. "You'll need the blessing of the tribe if you intend to go on Paiute land without desecrating it," she said. "Call Shaman Mahkah. Tell him I sent you."

Mayer examined the paper, the name and phone number of the Shaman scribbled upon it.

"Finish your tea," Theodosia said as she left the room.

Mayer knew why she wanted him to finish the tea. It was the same reason she gave it to him in the first place— she wanted to read the leaves. It wasn't the best chaser to a shot of rum, but Mayer knew not to tempt Theodosia, so he finished the drink, leaving the requisite teaspoon or so in the bottom of the cup.

When Theodosia returned and had taken her seat, Mayer pushed the teacup and saucer across the table to her. She took the teacup in her left hand and swirled the remaining liquid counter-clockwise. Then she said something quietly that Mayer did not understand and turned the cup over onto the saucer. After a minute or so, she turned it upright and gazed into the cup.

Mayer waited.

Theodosia concentrated on the leaves, but said nothing. She took the cup in her hand and turned it, holding it up to the light coming in from the kitchen's only window, but still did not speak.

"What is it?" Mayer finally asked.

Theodosia looked at Mayer intently. "Must you take this case?" she asked.

"I've already accepted the scratch," Mayer said. "And something definitely isn't kosher with that crime scene. Why? What do you see?"

"A wolf," Theodosia said.

"I thought the wolf was a symbol of loyalty?"

"It is. But it is also the symbol of destruction and death. Sunkmanitu, the Devine Dog, will one day chew through his chains and devour the sun at the end of times. Your wolf is baring its teeth, ready to attack. The leaves reveal danger ahead."

"Is that all?" Mayer asked.

"There is an H. At the tip of the wolf's teeth is the letter H."

"You think a wolf killed Hawthorne?" Mayer asked. "There are no wolves in Las Vegas."

Theodosia gave him a disapproving glare. "The wolf is only symbolic. It does not mean a wolf killed Hawthorne. It means there is danger in what you seek to do. The wolf is baring its teeth. If you proceed, it will bare them at you and you will be in grave danger."

Mayer stood. "It wouldn't be the first time," he said.

Mayer replaced his lid, kissed Theodosia on the cheek, and slid her a sawbuck. Then he turned to leave.

"Do not take this warning lightly, Prometheus," Theodosia warned. "It could be your undoing."

Mayer nodded, but he didn't look back.

9

MAYER RETURNED TO Atomic Liquors, parking in the back, the weight of Theodosia's words still weighing on him like a rain-soaked overcoat. The cards had told the truth. They always did, even if Mayer didn't want to hear it—or admit it.

He popped open his trunk and reached inside to the plain wood box he stored there, a box which housed his most valuable possession—his mother's diary. Mayer could have found some way to get to college, to earn a degree or two, maybe even pick up where his parents left off, but why? What would it have gained him? His knowledge had come from the streets, and there was more in his mother's writings than in any college course he could ever have taken.

He cradled the leatherbound book in his right hand, the rosary tapping against it, as he stepped inside the tavern. When his eyes adjusted to the dimness, Mayer found Virginia, Stella's mother, behind the bar. She had on a dark blue, A-line, day dress with puffed shoulders— its white collar and sleeve bands matched the buttons that ran the length of the dress. Her time-worn face lit as he entered.

"Prometheus," she said. "There you are. Come, take a seat."

Virginia was like a mother to Mayer, assuming the role when his own disappeared. For her part, Virginia always treated Mayer like the son she never had, keeping him housed, fed and, on more than one occasion, out of trouble. The first time he got pinched and ended up in the can, it was Virginia who posted bail. And it was Virginia who took him to court to account for his deeds instead of trying to use her influence to get him out of the jam.

"Coffee?" she asked.

Mayer nodded, taking a seat at one of the stools and placing his lid on the bar. He would have asked for something stronger, but he didn't want to chance one of Virginia's famous disapproving looks. When she turned to get the coffee, Mayer slid the diary under his lid.

Virginia placed the cup and saucer in front of Mayer, then filled it with the dark steaming brew. He took a deep breath, letting the scent from the roasted beans seep into his lungs. The day had already been strange and the familiar smell was a welcome change. Virginia had given him no spoon on the saucer, nor was there sugar or cream. Just how he liked it, though he would have liked it better with a little Irish whiskey.

Virginia watched him take a sip, then smiled pleasantly. "That your mother's diary?" she asked.

Mayer swallowed hard, resisting the urge to spit out the liquid, and tried not to choke. He should have known he wouldn't get anything past his surrogate mother; she was as keen-eyed as his own. "It is," he admitted, after composing himself.

Virginia raised a judgmental eyebrow. "Stella tells me you have a new case."

"Stella has a big mouth," Mayer said, then tried the coffee again. It went down much smoother the second time.

Virginia chuckled the way mothers do. "That why you have the diary?"

He nodded.

"The secrets to life are not in those pages, Prometheus."

"I wouldn't be so sure."

Virginia leaned over the bar and lifted Mayer's hat, exposing the book. She rubbed her hand gently over the soft cover. "I miss her, you know. Doris was more like a sister to me than a friend."

Mayer nodded.

"She had a way of seeing things. A way of looking inside a person and recognizing the truth."

Mayer flashed her a knowing smile and took another sip of coffee. "Theodosia claims I'm holding onto fear and pain," he said. "That I have to forgive myself."

"You went to see that gypsy again?" Virginia asked. It was accompanied by one of those looks he'd been trying to avoid, and more than a hint of vinegar.

"I know. You don't approve."

"Doris sought her advice all the time, and look where it got her?"

Mayer wrapped his hands around the plain white cup, taking in its warmth. He didn't respond.

Virginia placed a soft hand on Mayer's arm. "I'm sorry," she said. "That was uncalled for."

Mayer moved his hand atop hers and gave her a kind smile.

"I hate to say it," Virginia said, "but that gypsy is right, this time. You hold far too much guilt. What did you think a 17-year-old could do anyway?"

Mayer shrugged. He'd become dismissive of his parents once he entered high school—embarrassed by them. How do you explain that your parents are into the occult? *Not as followers*, he'd say, *just studying*. Yeah right. At some point, he had stopped having deep conversations with his mother, finding her opinions trivial and old fashioned. She had tried to continue them, but Mayer had resisted.

His parents were simply strange. Sure, it was easy to chalk it up to just the angst of a teenager, but he had purposely tried to avoid them. In fact, on the day they left for Germany—on the day they left his life forever—where was he? Off with his friends, smoking, looking at a nudie magazine, teasing a girl, or doing some other silly, frivolous activity. Something that didn't amount to a hill of beans.

"Where'd you go?" Virginia asked.

"Nowhere," Mayer lied, but they both knew he had drifted off.

"What's this case about?" Virginia asked.

"R. J. Hawthorne's Dutch act," Mayer said. "Though his partner doesn't believe Hawthorne capable of putting a pill in his own temple."

"And what do you think?"

"I guess I'm suspicious as well. Especially after my visit to Vera Krupp's place today."

Virginia looked taken aback. "You visited Vera Krupp?" she asked, though it seemed more like an accusation than a question.

"I did," Mayer confirmed.

"Is she involved in this?"

"It looks that way," Mayer said. "Although how she's involved, I don't yet know."

Virginia's eyes narrowed and somehow seemed to darken. Creases formed at their edges and her mouth tightened. "You mustn't take this case," she said forcefully.

"Too late, I've already accepted the scratch."

"Then give it back," she said quickly.

"Hey, what's going on here?" Mayer asked. He knew both the look Virginia was giving him, and the disapproval it represented.

"Nothing," Virginia said and turned away.

Her reluctance to answer surprised Mayer. "It's a little late for that," he said. "If you know something . . ." He let the sentence trail off. And then it hit him. "Is this about my parents?" he asked.

Virginia turned back to Mayer, her face solemn. She picked up the journal and turned the pages until she found what she was looking for. Then she placed the book in front of Mayer and pointed to a drawing on one of the pages. It was labeled *The Seal of the Seven Archangels*.

"I don't understand," Mayer said. "What does this have to do with Vera Krupp?"

"You know she was married to Alfried Krupp?"

"That's the rumor," Mayer said.

"Alfried Krupp of Hitler's war machines?"

"I'm aware of who Alfried Krupp is."

"Did you also know Krupp was a chief supporter of Hitler's delusions with the occult?"

"That I did not know," Mayer admitted.

"Your parents had a lead on the actual amulet that drawing represents, that's why they went to Germany."

"And how do you know this?" Mayer asked.

Virginia lowered her head and slowly began rubbing her hands together. Mayer had seen it before. It was what Virginia did when she was contemplating options. He should have given her time, but he didn't. Instead he pressed her.

"Tell me what you know," he said.

Virginia raised her head. Her large brown eyes were floating in a liquid of sadness, a redness beginning to overtake the whites. "Your mother wrote me letters regularly," she confessed.

The news hit Mayer like a fastball to the gut. "You have letters from my mother?" he asked. "And you never showed them to me?"

She nodded quietly.

As Mayer sat motionless, Virginia disappeared into the office, returning a short time later with a small bundle of envelopes tied together with twine. She laid the bundle on the bar next to Mayer.

"Doris kept me updated on all they were doing," she said. "She and Elias went to Germany because they had a lead on that amulet. They needed to find it before Hitler did. She wrote me when she could," she paused. "Then suddenly the letters stopped."

"And you're just telling me this now?" Mayer said a bit louder than he expected. Though there weren't many patrons in the place at this time of day, the few present turned their attention to the bar. That is, until Mayer flashed them a warning look and they returned to their own glasses.

Virginia's face softened and she lowered her voice. "What would you have done with this information, Prometheus?" she asked. "You needed to follow your own path in life, choose your own way."

"How's that worked out for me?"

Virginia took her time to answer, her words measured. "Vera Krupp recently moved into this valley. If you're going to involve her in this, it's better you know the whole story."

"It was Hawthorne who involved her, not me," Mayer said, smartly.

"Still, you're both now involved."

"Are you saying Alfried Krupp had the amulet?"

"Your mother thought so. Your father was a bit more skeptical."

Mayer remained quiet, letting the news bounce around his brain. Trying not to feel betrayed. "What else haven't you told me?" he asked.

Virginia walked around the bar and came over to Mayer. She reached out her arms, but Mayer's mood had soured. He picked up the letters, took hold of the diary, and replaced his lid. "A secret is no better than a lie," he said and stormed out.

Virginia called for him, but Mayer didn't turn back.

10

HE'D MADE IT about three steps out of the bar before he collided with Hank Greenspun's cub reporter.

"Watch where you're going," he barked.

"Well howdy do to you too," Cassi replied. She was dressed in the same high-waisted brown slacks and white, long-sleeve, button-down blouse she'd worn earlier, though now it seemed a bit disheveled. Her purse was flung over her right shoulder and the eraser end of a pencil stuck out above her ear. She was cradling a stack of mimeographed sheets of paper against her chest and she almost dropped them when the two collided.

Mayer stopped. He sighed. "What are you doing here?" he asked.

"Looking for you," Cassi admitted.

"Look Miss Reyes, I've tried to tell you . . ."

Cassi cut him off. "I've been doing some research," she said. "Do you have any idea how many people have disappeared or have been found dead in the area where the resort was to be built?"

Mayer had to admit that he did not.

Cassi adjusted the bundle of papers in her arms. "I've been at the library and the sheriff's department all afternoon. And you'll be simply amazed at what I've found. If we can just go back inside for a moment."

"That's no good," Mayer said.

Cassi screwed up her courage. "Look, Mr. Mayer, I've done a lot of work here and . . ."

Mayer cut her off with his hand. "Follow me," he said and took her to the back of Atomic Liquors where he had parked his Hornet. He motioned for her to lay the stack of papers on the hood. "Spill it," he said. "You've got ten minutes."

Mayer watched as Cassi spread out the mimeographed sheets. "Since 1924 there have been no less than twenty-five deaths or disappearances in the area where the resort was to be built," she said. "Some of them dismemberments."

"It's the desert," Mayer said. "People die out there all the time."

"Not like this," Cassi continued. "Almost every one of them had plans to build or settle on that site." She picked up one of the sheets, a duplication of a news clipping from the *Las Vegas Age* dated June 12, 1924.

DEVELOPER FOUND DISMEMBERED

Developer Ronald W. Spence was found dismembered yesterday in the Charleston Forest Reserve near the Sandstone Ranch. Spence was the main partner in a development deal to build ranch estates in the region. His body, according to Sheriff Sam Guy, was found by two men hiking in the area. "Darndest thing I ever saw," said Guy. "They was torn to shreds. Must have been coyotes or a mountain lion." The project is to be discontinued in light of Spence's untimely death.

Cassi pulled out another sheet, this one from the *Las Vegas Review Journal*, dated December 16, 1937.

LOCAL MAN DISAPPEARS

Samuel Johnathan Boatman has been missing for several days. His whereabouts unknown, according to his wife, Janet. She reported her husband missing after he failed to return from a trip to the Charleston Forest Reserve near the Sandstone Ranch, according to Sheriff Gene Ward. Boatman went with his surveyor, Walter Shannon, to survey the area in anticipation of building a cattle ranch. The two men left early Monday morning and have not been seen since. "I just don't know where he could have gone," Janet Boatman said. Sheriff Ward would not say if foul play was suspected; however, a search of the area produced no clues into the disappearance.

"There's more just like these," Cassi said. "All unsolved. Sometimes the men were simply missing and at other times they were found, ripped apart as if by animals, but almost all of them were connected by plans to develop in the area. And every single time the development plans ended with the death of the developer."

"What do you mean almost all of them?"

"There was one strange report of a set of twins that were missing from a family who lived in Blue Diamond. But they were toddlers, far too young to have development ties to the area, and their father wasn't a developer. He worked in the gypsum mine."

Mayer placed his foot on the bumper and leaned in. He studied the reports Cassi had found. She was right, one after the other, to a man, there was a tie to development in the area. Many of the men were never found, some committed suicide, while others were horribly dismembered. Each time the death marked the end of the development.

"It doesn't fit," Mayer said aloud.

"What doesn't fit?"

"The deaths, they're all different. There seems to be no consistency. Sometimes the bodies are found, sometimes they aren't. Sometimes they're torn apart, sometimes they're just missing."

"That's why I did some cross checking," Cassi said. "I found no incidences of people being mauled by animals in the surrounding area. At least none that weren't related to development near Sandstone Ranch, or whatever it was called at the time. There's no way this is a coincidence. Somebody doesn't want development in that area."

Mayer agreed, but he didn't let her know he'd stopped believing in coincidences long ago. "If somebody was killing these people," he said, "what message were they trying to send?"

"That's what I wondered."

Mayer remembered the hairs he found on the trailer floor. "The maulings make me wonder if we aren't dealing with..."

"Please don't say werewolf," Cassi said.

"Why not?"

"Don't be silly. Werewolves don't really exist."

Mayer let out a soft snort. "Every legend has some element of truth," he said.

Cassi scoffed. "Are you trying to tell me werewolves are real?"

"Werewolves, werecats, werehyenas. They may not be running wild, but, yes, they do exist," Mayer assured her. "Just not in the way you think. Though I haven't heard of one in Las Vegas for quite some time."

Cassi's eyes widened. "We've had werewolves in Las Vegas?"

"Sure," Mayer said. "I used to drink out of the same bottle with one of them. Until, well, you know."

Cassi didn't seem to know what to say. Mayer turned back to the sheets laid out on his hood. "But it doesn't work out," he said. "It doesn't explain Hawthorne killing himself."

"Maybe he shot himself before the, um, werewolf could get him," Cassi offered.

"Could be, but that doesn't explain the suicide note," Mayer said.

"What's your next move?" Cassi asked.

Mayer placed his loafer back on the ground and began stacking the sheets again, one on top of the other. "That, my dear, is none of your business. Thank you for this research, but how can I say this nicely?" he paused, then stepped closer to the newshawk. "Stay out of my way."

After Mayer finished stacking the sheets, he took them to the rear of the car and popped the trunk.

Cassi followed, determined. "I have no intention of staying out of this. And I'll thank you to give me back my papers," she said with an outstretched arm.

Mayer ignored her.

"I'm going to be involved, Mr. Mayer, one way or the other, so you can accept that and let me work with you, or . . ."

Mayer dropped the sheets in the trunk. He put the diary back in its spot—added the letters—and slammed the trunk. "Or what?" he demanded.

"Or . . ."

Cassi probably said some other things as well, but Mayer had stopped listening. Theodosia's words were ringing in his ears: *In order to succeed, you must do something you do not enjoy. Work as a team.*

He looked at the reporter intently. "Get in," he said.

The surprise showed on her face. "Where are we going?" she asked.

"Does it matter?"

11

FIVE MINUTES LATER the pair was being shown to a booth in Christie's Dining Room at the Hotel El Cortez by a blonde doll all smiles in a red pin-waist dress with a black point collar and armbands. Matching buttons marched in a line down her front. Cassi slipped herself into the booth as the waitress came up behind her and dealt out menus before scurrying away.

"Order me a rum on the rocks and whatever you want," Mayer said without taking a seat. "I'll be right back."

"Where are you going?" Cassi asked.

"Always the newshawk," Mayer said. "Well, if you must know, I've gotta make a call to finalize the evening's entertainment."

Mayer walked out of the restaurant and into the casino. The sounds of coins dropping and machines dinging and donging assaulted his senses. Casinos were noisy places, filled with people desperate to make an easy buck. Yelling with excitement after winning twenty-five cents on a penny machine, having put in fifty cents to get it. He didn't care much for casinos or the people in them, but he wasn't about to take Cassi to his favorite diner, so Christie's would have to do. Besides, it was just up the street, easy to get to.

Mayer headed to the concierge desk. "You got a blower I can borrow for a bit?" he asked.

A dusty, gray-haired relic from the Civil War with a long chin and a thin, angled mustache looked down his nose at Mayer. "Are you a guest here, sir?" he asked.

"No, but you can use the thing before I do to call Mr. Smith and tell him P. M. Mayer wants to use his phone, if you're keen on seeing what that gets you."

The relic gave Mayer the eye. Mayer gave it right back.

"Follow me," the man finally said and took Mayer to a quiet room, just off the main check-in desk. Mayer didn't like to drop names—unless he needed to—but he didn't mind using Jack Smith's name. The general manager of the El Cortez was a good friend of Virginia's and often came to Atomic Liquors after hours to relax. The fact that the two businesses were in walking distance from one another didn't hurt.

It was Jack's idea to rid the place of the pirate theme it suffered under Bill Moore, eliminating such notable hotspots as the Buccaneer Bar and Pirate's Den—the latter of which was decorated with elaborate depictions of female picaroons painted by Denny Stephenson. Mayer wasn't the only one who thought it a bit much. Not that he had anything against pirates, or picaroons for that matter, it just seemed like a strange theme for a hotel and gambling joint in the middle of the desert.

Mayer pulled the paper Theodosia had given him out of his pocket and picked up the business end of the blower. He dialed the number and waited. When the male voice came on the other end, Mayer introduced himself and quickly added that he'd been given the shaman's number by Theodosia.

"Yes, she is a good friend," the shaman said.

"I was wondering if you had some time this evening for a chat. I have something I'd like to run by you."

"Is it important?"

"Deadly," Mayer said.

"Got a pen and paper?"

The two men set a time, after which the shaman gave detailed directions to his home. Mayer put down the receiver and headed back to the café, tipping his hat to the relic as he passed. He slid into the booth, removed his lid, and took a sip of the rum Cassi had ordered for him. The pink squirrel she'd ordered for herself was already halfway gone.

"All set?" she asked.

"All set," Mayer assured her.

When the waitress returned, Cassi ordered the shrimp salad the menu assured her was "fresh." Mayer ordered the grilled pork chops and applesauce, with a rum chaser.

Cassi wrinkled her nose.

Mayer had been trying so hard to avoid the cub reporter that he never really got a good look at her. She was striking, in a girl-next-door sort of way. She had a button nose, a thin upper lip, and just enough gumption to get the job done. Her brown eyes sparkled above her high, round cheeks and her lips were painted a light shade of coral. She didn't wear rouge the way some women do, slapping it on like war paint. No, hers was very light over the upper cheekbone, and her arching eyebrows gave her a very natural look.

"What made you change your mind?" she asked.

"Who said that I have?"

She crinkled her nose again. It was probably meant to be dismissive, but it didn't come off that way. "So what does P. M. really stand for?" she asked.

"Portly man," Mayer responded.

Cassi twisted her mouth. "Cute," she said.

"How'd you find out about the will?"

Cassi stiffened. She pulled a pack of ivory-tipped Marlboros from her purse, slipped one in her mouth, and lit the end. She inhaled deeply, then let the smoke out the side of her mouth, like the French ladies do. "I didn't know there was a will," she said curtly.

"Come now, we both know that isn't true."

She nervously flicked the tip of the cigarette into the ashtray she had scooted in front of her. "I'm a reporter," she said. "I have sources."

"Very good ones, apparently."

"So it is true?" Cassi asked, doing little to hide her surprise.

"Sure it's true."

"Is that why you went to Vera Krupp's place after you left this afternoon?"

Mayer was impressed. "What do you know about our Mrs. Krupp?" he asked.

Cassi pulled the Stenopad from her purse, satisfying Mayer's curiosity as to where she'd kept it hidden. She opened the cover and flipped the pages until she found what she wanted. "Well," she began, "I know her name is Martha Vera Wilhelmine Hossenfeldt and she was born in Düsseldorf, Germany in 1909, an only child. She attended the best private school and, of course, had access to home tutors. After graduation, she attended the Sorbonne in Paris and the University of Frankfurt, studying history, French literature, medieval art, architecture and literature."

Mayer whistled. "Quite a spread."

"She did some modeling in her early years, using her first husband's last name of von Langen, then she divorced him in the mid-1930s and went on to become a successful actress in Berlin. I was able to see some photos of her from that time and she was quite the looker."

"I imagine she was," Mayer said. "Go on."

"When the war broke out in 38, she emigrated to America, was married and divorced," she looked up from her pad, then added, "Twice." She flipped a page and continued. "She also became a naturalized citizen. In 1951 she moved back to Germany to care for her ailing mother, where she was reunited with a childhood friend, Alfried, the man who would become her fourth husband on May 19, 1952. She moved back to America, or more specifically, Las Vegas, in 1955, after her mother's death, and bought Bar Nothing Ranch, which she then renamed Diamond V Ranch. As far as I can tell, she actually runs the ranch, working just as hard as her hands. Even brands calves."

Mayer thought back to his earlier meeting, when he shook Vera Krupp's hand and how it felt like that of a woman who didn't shy away from hard work. "Doesn't surprise me," he said.

"It also doesn't seem like they had much of a marriage at all. Alfried's family was wealthy, perhaps she was drawn to that."

"A gold digger?" Mayer asked. "Doesn't strike me as the kind."

"She does have a habit of cycling through husbands," Cassi said matter-of-factly.

She had a point.

Cassi closed her pad and smiled smugly. "Rumor has it she is currently seeking a divorce." She was about to continue when the waitress came with their food.

"Can I get you anything else?" she asked.

Mayer held up his empty rum glass. "I'll take another of these."

Cassi declined a second.

When the waitress left, Mayer turned to his companion. "What would happen if you lost that Stenopad?" he asked.

"Do you want to hear more, or are you just going to be smart?"

Mayer motioned for her to continue.

"Apparently, infidelity is involved."

"Is that so?"

Cassi nodded, then took a forkful of salad.

"Do tell."

Cassi chewed a minute then continued. "There have been reports of a gentleman caller at the ranch. The couple has been seen riding off on two of Vera's horses, at times not returning until very late in the evening."

"You don't say." Mayer said as he cut his chops.

Cassi stopped and narrowed her eyes. "Hey, are you playing me for a sap?" she asked.

"No," Mayer lied. "Just trying to get the angle." Truth was that Mayer wanted to know what Cassi knew and, if he could find out, how she knew it. While he remembered Theodosia's words, it didn't mean he'd accepted them. It also didn't mean he had to work with a newshawk.

"Okay," Mayer said. "So you've done your homework. Now tell me how you knew about the will? That information wasn't released and no one else knew anything about it."

Cassi hesitated. "Give me that interview I've been asking for," she said, "and I'll tell you."

"Pound sand," Mayer said.

Cassi slumped. "Oh, don't be that way. You've got to give me something here."

The waitress returned with Mayer's drink.

Cassi waited for her to leave, then continued. "I'll start," she said. "I know your father's name is Elias Mayer and your mother's name is Doris."

"Was," Mayer said.

"Excuse me?"

"Was," he repeated. "That was my father's name and it was my mother's name."

"Oh," Cassi said. "I'm sorry. I had no idea."

Mayer spoke before she could continue. "My parents were paranormal investigators who worked for the government. My mother was from California. She went to school there, studying Greek Mythology and Occult Studies at Berkley. She graduated with a Ph.d. My father was from Germany. He left there with his family when the Great War broke out. He met my mother in California and they married. I was born here."

"How did they . . ." Cassi dropped the question when Mayer flashed a warning glare. She let the mood settle before trying another. "Why do you wear the onyx on your left wrist?"

"The ancient Egyptians believed a vein ran from the third finger of the left hand directly to the heart. The Romans called it the vena amoris. Onyx is a healing stone. On the left wrist, it protects that vein, and, therefore, the body."

"Is that true?"

"I don't know. I'm not a doctor."

Mayer didn't want to reveal that the real reason he wore the bracelets was because he was told to do so by Theodosia. That he really didn't know the reason, except that Theo told him that onyx was indeed a healing stone, and if Theo told him to do it, then that's what he did.

"And the rosary? Are you Catholic?"

"Religion is mostly invented by men," Mayer said, "but the rosary has been blessed by a priest and it never hurts to cover your bets."

Cassi smiled. "What about the tattoo? I've never seen a symbol like that before."

Mayer glanced at his right arm. His sleeve had moved up just enough to reveal the Icelandic symbol. It had been a part of him for so long, that he often forgot it was there.

"It's the Helm of Awe," he said, "also known as the Helm of Terror. It was taken from the dragon by Sigurd, after he slayed the beast." Mayer paused, then continued. "That's all I'm willing to tell you, Miss Reyes. It's all you need to know."

The two sat in silence for several minutes, eating their respective meals.

"An old boyfriend," Cassi finally said.

Mayer looked up.

"An old boyfriend of mine works in the sheriff's department. He let me see the note."

"He the one who told you about the gentleman caller?"

Cassi nodded.

"I don't suppose he mentioned the goose's name?"

"He doesn't know it. Only sees them on patrol."

Mayer nodded. It would appear past loves could come in handy.

"Let me ask you one final question," Cassi said. "Why would R. J. Hawthorne leave his part of the project to Vera Krupp?"

"Well that's the question, isn't it?" Mayer answered. "Finish up, we have another stop to make."

12

MAYER PAID THE bill, tipped the waitress, and escorted Cassi back to his Hornet. Then he drove twenty miles east following the directions the shaman had given him. At one point he was forced to abandon the paved road in favor of a dirt one. Cassi held tight to the dashboard, Mayer the steering wheel, as they bounced down the trail, driving past each landmark the shaman had identified—sometimes an odd-looking cactus, other times a distinct Joshua Tree—until he found a small, unassuming adobe house nestled in the heart of nowhere, the only house for miles. Not quite the end of the world, but Mayer was pretty sure he could see it from here.

The sun disappearing on the horizon cast an orange hue over the rolling clouds. Cassi got out of the passenger's side and slung her purse over her shoulder. Mayer joined her.

"Where have you taken us?" Cassi asked.

"Just you let me do the talking," he said, straightening his lid.

Cassi followed Mayer to the wooden front door, one that looked more like it belonged on the front of an old mission than a man's home. There was no doorbell to ring, no knocker to knock. Instead, a brass bell with a long, leather string hanging down from the clanker was secured to the adobe wall. Mayer gave it a hard swing. Then another for good luck.

A dog barked.

A light lit.

The door creaked open, swollen from the summer heat.

"You must be Mayer," the old man on the other side of the door said. He wore a Hawaiian shirt, covered by a brown leather vest. Two beaded necklaces peeked out from under the collar. He was a man much older than Mayer, his once black hair having turned all but completely gray. Except for his eyebrows. Although there were splashes of the color that had overtaken his crown, they were still mostly black. And while the marks of age had embedded themselves in his face, especially around the eyes, they somehow remained youthful and bright. "And you've brought a young lady with you." He smiled. "Theodosia said you wouldn't be alone."

A brown and gray dog, with two different colored eyes, poked his head out from between the door and the frame. He sniffed Mayer's pant leg, looked up at the man, and growled. Then he turned his attention to Cassi, wagging his tail.

"Won't you come in?" the shaman said. "Don't worry. Diogie won't bite."

Mayer and Cassi stepped inside. The shaman walked easily behind them. "Have a seat," he said.

Three chairs were set in a manner that allowed their occupants to face each other. A side table was set between two of the chairs, which were placed a bit closer together to each other than to the third. Mayer removed his lid as he entered and placed it on the table.

"Can I get you something to drink?" the shaman asked. "I have tea."

"Earl Grey?" Mayer asked.

"Prickly pear," the shaman answered.

"I'll pass."

"Where are my manners?" the shaman said. He walked over to Cassi and held out his hands. "Thank you for coming to my home, my dear. I'm called Mahkah, and I am at your service."

Cassi placed her hands in his. "I'm Cassi Reyes," she said. "Pleased to meet you."

The shaman gave her a toothy smile. "Short for Cassandra, I imagine."

"Cassiopeia, actually," she said.

That caught Mayer's attention. He had made the same assumption as the shaman—one that was clearly wrong.

"Aw, the wife of Cepheus," the shaman said, "who was transformed into a constellation, lighting the northern sky. Fitting."

Cassi's face lit up. "That's right," she said. "And what does your name mean?"

The shaman led her to one of the chairs and motioned for her to take a seat. "Earth," he said. "Though it seems a bit of an imperious name for one man to carry. Will you take some tea?"

"Yes," she said.

While the shaman made the tea, Mayer had a quick look around. Besides the usual trappings of chairs, tables, and lamps, there were also items that seemed particular to the home of a medicine man. Amethyst, bloodstone, carnelian, and other crystals Mayer didn't recognize rested between books of Greek, Roman, French, English, and American literature. Shaman Mahkah was clearly well read.

A collection of apothecary herbs were laid out on one of the tables—some in dark brown bottles and others in tied bunches. Next to the collection of herbs were several mortars and pestles, as well as decorative bowls. A small bundle of sage, its end burnt, rested in one of the bowls, along with an assemblage of various totems.

The shaman returned with two cups of tea. He handed one to Cassi and set the other on a small table next to the offset single chair. Instead of taking the seat, the shaman instead picked up the bundle of sage and struck a match. He lit the end and allowed the sage to burn until it began to smoke.

He held the sage up high above his head. "Sacred and holy ones," he began, "please clear this home of evil and negative energy so that we may commune in peace." Then he lowered the sage to his mouth and blew the smoke into the air, using his free hand to assist with the spreading. He walked over to Cassi first and slowly moved the sage around her head and body.

The dog came over to Cassi and laid his head on her lap. "Diogie likes you," the shaman said. "He's a very good judge of character."

"Such an unusual name," Cassi said. "Does it mean something in Paiute?"

"No, the shaman admitted. "His name is simply Diogie. D. O. G."

Mayer laughed. Cassi flashed him a look.

When he was done with Cassi, the shaman returned to the table and tapped the sage into the bowl where it had once rested to release the ashes. He motioned for Mayer to take a seat, then performed the same ritual he had done with his companion, though he seemed to linger longer than he had with her. "There is much energy in you," he said as he passed the sage over Mayer's head.

"Negative?" Mayer asked.

"Some," the shaman responded. "More than there should be."

"Dandy."

When the shaman finished, he returned the sage to the bowl, letting it burn, and took his seat. "Now," he said as he picked up his tea, "how can I be of assistance?"

Mayer sat upright in his chair and asked, "Are you familiar with R. J. Hawthorne?"

The shaman allowed himself a quick grin. "Of course I am. All Paiutes are familiar with the man who intended to build a resort on sacred land."

"Then you know he offed himself last night?"

"I am aware the man took his own life, yes."

"You don't seem terribly shook up about it."

"Everyone has their own path in life, Mr. Mayer. Surely you understand that. Mr. Hawthorne simply followed his chosen path."

"Not everyone sees it that way, and I'm beginning to wonder myself." Mayer went on to explain what he had found at the trailer. The missing holes in the wall, the reloading of the revolver, the hairs he found on the floor, and the hawk with the red eyes that seemed to follow him. He intentionally left out anything about Vera Krupp, the will, and the housekeeper who worked for both of them.

The shaman listened intently as he sipped his tea. "Do you have the hairs?" he asked.

Mayer removed the handkerchief from his pocket, opened it to reveal the hairs he'd taken from the floor of the trailer, then handed it to the shaman. The shaman opened the handkerchief and brought the hairs to his nose.

"Coyote," he said. He took another sniff and twisted his face a bit. Then he took some of the hairs and brought them over to the table that held his herbs, totems, and bowls. He dropped the hairs into a bowl, then opened a bottle containing a reddish powder. He tapped the powder into the same bowl and watched. An orange smoke began to rise slowly, then grew stronger, ending with a bright puff.

"That can't be good," Mayer said.

"It is not good," the shaman said over his shoulder. "Black magic." He moved the bowl over to the smoking sage and let it rest. He turned to Mayer. "You say you saw a hawk with red eyes?"

"Well, I think it was a hawk," said Mayer. "It could have been any type of large bird."

The shaman took his seat. He folded the handkerchief and returned it to Mayer.

"I thought werewolf at first, but it doesn't fit," said Mayer. "And I don't know where the hawk fits in."

"I think I might," the shaman said. "Though, if it is what I'm thinking, you're not far off."

13

THE SHAMAN REACHED to the side of his chair and brought up a soft leather drawstring pouch. He pried open the strings, reached in, and took out a homemade pipe, which he then filled with what Mayer assumed was tobacco from the same pouch. But it could have been prickly pear, Mayer wasn't certain. He tapped down the substance, then pulled a match from the table, snapped it alive with the nail of his thumb and lit the pipe. He drew in several deep breaths before the thing took. Once he was satisfied with his efforts, he spoke.

He blew a puff of smoke into the space above his head, then asked, "Have you ever heard of naagloshii or yee naaldooshi?"

"Can't say that I have," Mayer admitted.

"Maybe you'd know it by its English name—skinwalker."

"Skinwalker?" Cassi repeated. "What on Earth is that?"

The shaman addressed Cassi. "A skinwalker is the Native American version of a werewolf," he said.

"Oh, bother!" Cassi exclaimed. "Now there's two of you."

Mayer hooked his thumb at Cassi. "She doesn't believe in werewolves."

The shaman grinned. "There is an element of truth in every legend," he said to Cassi.

She crinkled her nose. "You sound just like him," she said with an accusatory finger.

"Can you tell me about this skinwalker?" asked Mayer.

The shaman rested the pipe in a bowl on the table next to him. Then he pressed his hands together as if he were praying, and brought them to his lips. He looked ahead, but not at anything in particular. Diogie left Cassi and moved over to the shaman. He laid down by his legs, but kept a weather eye on Mayer.

Mayer waited.

After several long and quiet minutes the shaman focused his deep, dark eyes on Mayer. "What you are asking is something that should not be discussed with outsiders," he said. "Navajos fear the skinwalker so much that they will not even speak of the creature in their own homes. They especially will not speak of it to an outsider. In fact, most refuse to even utter the word at night for fear of retaliation. They believe just talking about the naagloshii can bring one upon you."

"Speak of the devil and he doth appear," Mayer said softly.

"Exactly," the shaman agreed.

"And you?" Mayer asked. "What do you believe?"

The shaman returned to his pipe. "I'm Paiute. We don't believe in skinwalkers."

"That didn't answer my question."

The shaman took a deliberate puff, weighing his response. "As I said before, there is an element of truth to all legends. But I do not believe this is one I should share with you. Outsiders tend to destroy native culture, especially white outsiders."

Mayer's face tightened. "Then why did you agree to a meeting?" he asked.

"Call it curiosity. Plus, Theodosia speaks highly of you."

Mayer let out a heavy breath.

"You can trust P. M.," Cassi offered.

"Oh?" the shaman said, "and how do you know this? Have you two not just recently met?"

Mayer didn't know how the shaman knew that and he didn't much care. He also didn't much like being jerked around. "Look, I'm no skid rogue, if that's what you're worried about. I'm square and I know how to keep secrets."

"And yet you brought a reporter to my home."

Mayer stood. "Come on Reyes," he said as he picked up his hat. "We're tooting the wrong ringer."

Diogie sat up and growled.

Cassi stood slowly. She looked to Mayer and then to the shaman.

Mayer was already three steps to the door when the shaman asked, "Why is it that you need this information? What do you plan to do with it?"

Mayer turned to the shaman. "Put all the pieces together for one. A man doesn't generally shoot six times, reload his heater, and then off himself. He doesn't write a death will leaving all his shares in a project to the woman who opposed him at every step. And he doesn't die with a frozen look of terror on his face if he did indeed plan to send his soul to the great beyond, or wherever your kind thinks the soul goes."

"That depends on which soul you mean," the shaman said. "My kind believe in two souls."

"Well isn't that just dandy?"

"And what is the second?" the shaman asked.

"Second?"

"You said 'for one,' which implies there is a second."

"There is," said Mayer. "If there's a killer on the loose, one who's already struck down one partner, then why wouldn't that killer attack the second partner as well? It's my responsibility to stop the thing from killing anyone else."

"Isn't that best handled by the police?"

"Not if it's a skinwalker," Mayer countered.

"And why is it your responsibility?"

"It just is, that's all."

The shaman turned to Cassi. "And you, what is your role in all this?"

Cassi tried a softer approach. "I'll admit, I'm looking for a story," she said. "But I'm not about to print anything about werewolves, skinwalkers, or wereanything for that matter. I'd be laughed off the paper. If Hawthorne killed himself, I want to know why and if he didn't, I want to know that too."

The shaman fiddled with his pipe, then reached down and scratched Diogie's scalp. The dog seemed pleased with the gesture. "Well, I suppose, if Theodosia trusts you." He paused. "Perhaps we should start again. Please, sit."

Mayer hesitated, but eventually did as requested, placing his lid back on the side table. Cassi sat as well.

"A skinwalker is a type of shapeshifter," the shaman began. "A witch who uses enchanted hides and feathers to become any animal it desires. This is why a Navajo will not wear the pelt of any predatory animal."

"So it could become a coyote?" asked Mayer.

"Yes," the shaman confirmed. "It can also become a wolf, a fox, a cougar, a bear, or even a dog."

Diogie looked up.

The shaman continued. "The witch uses the animal's natural abilities to its own advantage. If it needs strength and endurance, it might become the bear. If it needs speed, grace, and stealth, it might become the cougar. If it needs to follow someone unseen with keen vision or use sharp talons, it might become the crow, the eagle, the owl, or the hawk."

Mayer learned forward. "So you think my hawk might be one of these skinwalkers?" he asked.

"It is possible," the shaman confirmed. "You say the bird had glowing red eyes?"

"Like coals in a fire."

"That is one of the signs, but . . ." the shaman hesitated.

"But what?" Mayer pressed.

The shaman shook his head. "It doesn't make sense," he said. "Skinwalkers are Navajo, not Paiute. I have never heard of a Paiute becoming a skinwalker."

"Aren't there Navajos around here?"

"I suppose there could be. The Navajo people are comprised of the Pueblo, Apache, Hopi, and Ute. Some of these are our neighbors to both the northeast and the southeast."

Cassi interrupted. "Why do you call it a witch?"

The shaman puffed his pipe. "Spirituality is a natural part of life. It is in our history, our culture, and our traditions. We harness these powers in our medicine and for the good of our community. You do the same, do you not? Do you not pray to your god? Do you not believe miracles exist?"

"Well yes, but . . ."

"Just as with your religion, we believe there are places in this world where goodness is present, just as there are those surrounded by evil. The skinwalker is often a healer or spiritual guide who has turned. It seeks to direct the spiritual forces of nature to cause harm instead of good. It is no longer a healer, but a witch."

"So how do I kill it?" Mayer asked coldly.

"It's not that easy," the shaman said. "You are dealing with powerful black magic. In order to become a skinwalker, the witch must perform an unspeakable crime—killing a relative, often a child. It is evil to the core. A person with no redeeming value, possessed by greed, anger, envy, and spite—often revenge. A blackness has overtaken its heart and soul and it must continually kill, or perish itself."

The shaman took another puff. "The skinwalker can control the skin or body of man, read the mind, and use the secrets and fears that lie within to control a person. It can enter into its victim's own body, taking possession, and, in a sense, becoming that person. It can even mimic voices from the person's past."

Cassi scooted to the edge of her chair. "Does the person know?" she asked. "I mean, does he know he's being possessed?"

"Oh yes," the shaman confirmed. "The possessed is forced to watch in horror as the skinwalker makes him commit the most debased and defiled acts. All the while helpless to stop it."

Cassi shivered.

Mayer thought of Hawthorne, of the suicide note he left, the shot to the head ending his life, and of the terror painted on his face in the morgue. It was beginning to make sense.

The shaman continued. "The skinwalker can control the creatures of the night and use them to do his bidding. More powerful ones are able to call up the spirits of the dead and to reanimate corpses."

"How do I spot one of these skinwalkers?" Mayer asked.

"When in the animal form, it is larger and more powerful than the animal it has transformed into," the shaman said. "But it is not quite human and not quite animal. It is the eyes that will betray it. While in the animal form, the eyes will not look like an animal, but like a human. That is, until light shines upon them, then they turn bright red—like fire. Much like your hawk's eyes did when they caught the sun. When they are in human form, it is the opposite—their eyes look more like an animal than a human."

"So just look into the eyes?" asked Mayer.

"Yes, but not directly or it can control you. And if you see the face of a skinwalker, it has to kill you to prevent you from revealing its secret. This is why they are so dangerous."

"How do I kill it?" Mayer asked a second time.

"That is not easy," the shaman repeated. "A skinwalker is notoriously hard to kill. Regular bullets will simply have no effect, and of course, there's also corpse powder."

"Corpse powder." Mayer repeated bluntly.

"A dust composed of dried and powdered human remains," the shaman said. "If blown into your face, your tongue will turn black and begin to swell. Convulsions and paralysis will follow. If not treated, you will die."

"Dandy," Mayer said, then asked, "How does one go about making this corpse powder?"

"It is usually made from the bones of children, twins specifically," the shaman said.

Mayer looked to Cassi, her face registering her understanding.

"There are bone pellets as well," the shaman said.

"Do tell," said Mayer.

"The skinwalker will grind a bone down to the tiniest of pellets. It will curse the thing with chants, charms, and spells—all black magic. The pellet is then shot at its victim, usually with a blowgun. It imbeds itself into the skin, without leaving so much as a mark."

"And then what happens?" asked Cassi. though Mayer wasn't sure she wanted the answer.

"Social misfortune, sickness, and eventually, death." The shaman turned to Mayer. "Navajo law is quite clear in the matter. When a person becomes a skinwalker, he forfeits his humanity—his right to exist. For that reason, a skinwalker can be killed without legal or moral consequences."

"Great, but you haven't told me what I need to kill it with," said Mayer.

"Silver bullets dipped in white ash," the shaman said, "but you have to hit it while in animal form and only in the neck. If you shoot the thing in the neck, it will go into the human head and the skinwalker will die. Of course, you must find it first."

"And where does one find a skinwalker?"

"Someplace they can perform their ceremonial rites undisturbed. Typically in a dark cave or secluded place high in the hills. Often on or near sacred land."

"Then that's where I need to go," said Mayer.

"*We* need to go," Cassi corrected him.

Mayer gave her hard eyes, but eventually relented. "How do we go about getting permission to do that?" he asked the shaman.

"When would you like to go?"

"As soon as possible," Mayer said.

"It is not good to go at night," the shaman said. "That is when the skinwalker is most powerful. I will convene the elders. If they agree, we will meet you tomorrow, then bless your entrance onto our land."

"Can you meet me at the proposed resort?" Mayer asked.

"We can meet you near that area. Blessing must be given before you can step on sacred land."

"Do you think the elders will agree?"

"We shall see. Be there as the sun rises. If the elders have gathered, then they have agreed."

Mayer thanked the man and offered his hand. The shaman took it, then escorted him and Cassi to the door. Diogie followed, eyeing Mayer purposely.

"The task you intend to undertake is not wise," the shaman said. "It is not something you should do alone. Powerful magic is required to defeat black magic." He paused. "I must go with you."

"I can't ask you to do that," Mayer said.

"It is not something for which you can ask," the Shaman said. "It is the path I choose to follow. The one I must take."

Mayer nodded. He shook the shaman's hand a second time and was about to leave when another question came to him. "If Navajos won't speak about this, then how did you come to this knowledge?"

The shaman smiled, but did not answer.

Mayer and Cassi climbed into his Hornet and headed back down the dirt road the way they came. The dust created by the tires rose from the road and drifted high into the air. High enough, in fact, to almost reach the red-tailed hawk circling above.

14

THE TRIP BACK to Atomic Liquors was mostly quiet—Mayer thinking about all the day had brought, and Cassi—well he guessed Cassi was just trying to make sense of the whole thing. He took a spot behind the building.

"Now what?" Cassi asked.

"Now, you go home and go to bed. Meet me here before the cock crows and we'll go up into the hills and have a look-see."

Cassi nodded.

"You all right with all this?" Mayer asked.

She tried to show courage, but her face betrayed her. "I'm not sure. It's a lot to process. Is this what the Sloan Canyon incident was about?"

"Something like this, but not exactly."

Cassi moved her hand to the door handle. "What do you expect to find up there?"

Mayer shrugged. "I don't know. Could be a trip for biscuits for all I know."

Cassi nodded a second time. She opened the door and stepped out.

Mayer threw his arm over the back of the seat and leaned toward her. "If you're not here, I'm not waiting for you," he said.

"I'll be here," Cassi assured him, then shut the door harder than she should have.

Mayer watched as Cassi climbed into her own vehicle, a Ford Fairlane, powder blue on the top, white on the bottom, with whitewall tires and a hard roof. *Quite a car*, he thought to himself, noting that they must be paying better at the *Morning Sun* than he realized. He waited until she pulled out, then he headed west on Fremont Street, taking another left onto Second Street, crossing both Carson and Bridger Avenues. He pulled into the vacant lot behind a small church.

Las Vegas was deceptively quiet at this time of night. The summer air still. Off in the distance a train whistled and people, suitcases in hand, waited to board a bus headed anywhere out of town—longing for the life they once knew, or one better than they found here. An owl hooted from atop a perch on a worn telephone pole as shadows moved in a nearby alley. A lone streetlamp lit the church's parking lot and its single occupant.

Mayer got out of the car and closed the door behind him. He surveyed the area. Not that he was expecting to find anything, but it never hurt to check. In fact, it was one of the first things Mayer did every time he entered a building, or came to a new place. It was important to know how to escape if the need presented itself—which it often did.

Mayer opened the trunk and took out the diary. He slid it into his suit pocket and closed the trunk. Then he walked to the back of the modest church whose roots went nearly to the beginning of Las Vegas itself, starting as a wooden one-room building in 1909 and growing through the years to its current incarnation and its current pastor, Monsignor Devlin. It was he who gave Mayer the rosary he kept on his right wrist. "The right hand of God," according to the monsignor, was the place one should strive to remain. Mayer wrapped the rosary around his wrist to remind him where he was supposed to be, especially since he very seldom found himself there.

He made his way through the gate under the flagstone arch to the peaked wooden door at the rear of the church. He knew the monsignor would still be there, dressed in his black robes, on his knees, reciting his nightly prayers, and lighting a candle for people like him.

It took three knocks before the monsignor answered. "Prometheus," he said when he opened the door. "What brings you to the Lord's house at this time of night?"

"Hello Monsignor," said Mayer. "I have something for you to see. Something I hope you can tell me a little more about."

"Come in," the monsignor said and stepped aside.

Mayer removed his lid and went in. The monsignor took a last look around before closing the door behind him. "Come, have a seat," he said.

The diocese provided its priests with a small room to the rear of the church, a place where they could rest and do such things as ponder the meaning of life between services. Mayer walked over to the decorative wooden table that held an ornate lamp—a woman dressed in the full garb of a knight, sans helmet, held a torch high in her left hand, a shield to her back, and a dagger in her right. The patron saint of the church. A chair rested on each side. On the table in front of one of the chairs a book of poetry sat at the ready; a worn marker peeked out somewhere near the middle.

Mayer took the other seat and placed his lid on the table.

"I see you're still wearing the rosary around your wrist."

Mayer glanced at the prayer beads, then nodded.

"Well, will you have a smell from the barrel?"

"Sure, got any rum?" asked Mayer.

The monsignor chuckled. "No, but I do have some good Jameson I might share with you." He opened a cabinet and removed a well-used bottle, along with two small glasses. He poured the golden alcohol into both, added a bit more just for good measure, then pushed one of the glasses over to Mayer. Lifting his own glass, he said, "May you be in heaven a half an hour before the devil knows you're dead."

Mayer lifted his as well, then took a snort, enjoying the burn. "You know you're not Irish," he said.

"No, but the whiskey is," the monsignor said as he refilled the glasses.

"Do you ever drink anything but Irish whiskey?"

"Only on Sundays, my son." The monsignor took the seat across from Mayer. "Now what have you got for me?"

Mayer pulled the book from his pocket, opened the diary to the same place Virginia had earlier in the day, and set the book on the table in front of the monsignor. On the page was a drawing of a seven-pointed star encased in a double-bordered circle. Seven names, Mayer assumed where the archangels—Gabriel, Raphael, Simiel, Michael, Uriel, Iophiel, and Zachariel—were written around the circle, between the two borders. He did not recognize the other names and symbols, though many of them carried labels in his mother's handwriting.

"The Seal of the Seven Archangels," the monsignor said. "And quite a nice rendering of it, I might add."

"What can you tell me about it?"

"May I?" the monsignor asked, motioning to the book.

Mayer nodded.

He took the book in his hands, turned it over, and examined the cover. "Is this your mother's diary?" he asked.

Mayer nodded again. He'd spoken of the diary many times, but had never before shown it to the man who, like Theodosia, he'd come to see as a spiritual advisor. The two had become friends on accident, though Monsignor Devlin didn't see it that way, and perhaps he was right. Mayer had found the church after a particularly difficult night. Not that he was Catholic, he just needed a sanctuary, a place where he could escape the world, if only for a few moments. He'd sat in the pew for more than an hour when the monsignor came and sat with him.

Maybe it was the giant cross, the rows of lit candles, or the stained glass that got to him, or maybe it was the fact that priests, like lawyers, were sworn to secrecy, but Mayer began to confess to the priest. Not in the traditional Catholic way, but in a way that, nonetheless, unburdened his soul. To his credit, the monsignor didn't run away screaming or call the men with the white coats to come and fetch him. Instead he listened, quietly. He listened and nodded and the two men spoke of things seen and unseen in the world, as well as the seemingly eternal battle of good and evil. Mayer had come back many times since.

The priest turned the book back over and studied the page. "The names of the seven archangels are written in the circle surrounding the star," he began. "The smaller circle inside the star contains the seven luminaries—Sun, Moon, Mars, Mercury, Jupiter, Venus, and Saturn." He pointed to a set of symbols Mayer didn't recognize. "These symbols are the ten sefirot of the Kabbal. The ten creative forces that God uses to intervene between the infinite and the known world." Then he named them off, one by one: "keter elyon, halhma, bina, hesed, gevura, tif eret, netzah, hod, yesod, and malkhut."

He looked up at Mayer. "What is it that you need to know?"

"What those mean for one."

The monsignor chuckled. "They are the supreme crown, wisdom, intelligence, love, might, beauty, eternity, majesty, foundation, and kingship. Does that help?"

"Greatly," Mayer admitted.

"Anything else?"

"I was told today that my parents were searching for an amulet with this on it when they disappeared. Why would they be searching for this? What power does it contain?"

"I have heard of an amulet with this sigil on it," the monsignor said. "Supposedly forged in the fires of

Hades. The official stance of the church is simple: it is nonsense."

"Catholics don't believe in talismans?" Mayer asked. "Is that why I see so many St. Christopher medals in automobiles these days?"

The monsignor laid the diary down on the table. "Ah yes," he said. "The patron saint of travel and transportation. Do you know how he attained that position?"

"Something about carrying a child over a river."

"Something like that. One day a small boy approached Christopher as he was standing by a river and asked if he would carry him across. Christopher, being a very large man, saw no problem with the request and quickly honored it. Only, as Christopher progressed, the boy grew heavier and heavier, until the future saint could barely make it across. Once he made it to the other side, Christopher put the boy down on the bank and commented on how heavy the boy had become. The boy revealed that he was Jesus, and that he carried the weight of the world on his shoulders. Then the boy vanished."

The monsignor refilled their glasses. "Did you know that Christopher literally means 'Christ carrier? We do not worship saints, Mayer. We keep representations of them to remind us to ask them to intercede on our behalf before God."

"Talismans."

"These symbols are not talismans. They are not magic, nor do they provide good luck to the bearer, as does a rabbit's foot or four-leaf clover."

"I'm not sure the bird in his car sees them as any different."

"Perhaps not, but the belief behind them is vastly different."

"And what of this amulet then?"

The monsignor returned his attention to the diary. "Seven angels were created to be the watchers of men. Michael, Gabriel, and five others whose names are not as well known because they were removed from the canonical Bible at the Council of Rome in the fourth century."

"And these angels had special powers?"

"More than the typical angel, but not as much as people tend to think. There are nine types of angels, or as the church puts it, levels of hierarchy of the heavenly hosts: angels, archangels, principalities, powers, virtues, dominions, thrones, cherubim, and seraphim. Archangels are just slightly above angels. The legend behind the seven archangels is known as the "Myth of the Fallen Angels.""

"Fallen angels?" Mayer asked. "I thought Lucifer was the only fallen angel."

"Lucifer is certainly one of the fallen angels, but there are many others who followed him. These other fallen angels came to earth and are responsible for the evil that is here to this very day—much of which you are personally familiar. Angels such as Semihazah and Asael came to earth, took human wives, and birthed violent giants who sowed chaos and destruction. Worst of all, they taught the children of men many of heaven's secrets. It became so dire that Enoch rose to heaven in a flaming chariot to try and get Heavenly Father to intercede. This is how the seven came to be."

"To stop the giants?"

The monsignor nodded. "And the fallen," he said. "In the time of Noah, the seven archangels imprisoned the guilty angels and destroyed their offspring, after which the earth had to be cleansed."

"The flood," Mayer said.

"The flood," the monsignor repeated.

"So why would my parents be searching for this amulet if it truly holds no power, and why would my mother write what she did at the bottom of the thing?" Mayer pointed to the symbol on the page, at the bottom of which were written the words: *Hitler believes he can control the destroying angel with The Seal of the Seven Archangels.*

"That is because the amulet is believed to hold the power of the seven archangels—a power which can be used for both good and evil. Not officially, of course."

"Angels do evil?"

"Not evil, per se, but one of the seven is the Angel of Death mentioned in Exodus 12:23. 'For the Lord will pass through to smite the Egyptians; and when he seeth the blood upon the lintel, and on the two side posts, the Lord will pass over the door, and will not suffer the destroyer to come in unto your houses to smite you.'"

"Sounds ominous," Mayer said and took another snort. "So does this amulet have magic properties?"

"You know how I feel about magic."

"I know," Mayer said, then continued in his best imitation of the monsignor. "Magic is an attempt to make reality bend to the will of the user."

"People attempt to use such things as signs, sigils, and amulets to summon, influence, and control divine beings—including God," said the monsignor. "It is blasphemy. Delusional, heretical pride."

"So there's nothing to this amulet?"

"You know better than that, Prometheus. Hitler must have placed a great deal of importance on this amulet to have searched for it. Your parents must have done so as well or they would not have gone hunting for it either. The amulet creates a type of doorway between this world and the spirit world. It can be used to establish a communication link between the holder and the seven archangels. More specifically, the seal can be used to communicate with one archangel in particular."

"The Angel of Death."

"Exactly."

Mayer rubbed his whiskered chin and stared at the table.

"What is it, my son?"

"Virginia has been holding back information from me about my parents."

"I see."

"I knew they were working for the government and that they were focused on Hitler's obsession with the occult. I knew they disappeared in the line of duty, but until today, I didn't know why. I also did not know that my mother corresponded with Virginia, through letters, while she was in Germany."

"Virginia told you?"

Mayer nodded.

"But not before today?"

"Not even a whiff."

"Perhaps she was trying to protect you."

Mayer was indignant. "Protect me? By not showing me letters she had from my own mother?"

The monsignor's voice softened. "Letters are private things, Prometheus. She was under no obligation to show them to you."

"And what am I supposed to do now?"

"Where are these letters?"

"She gave them to me. I have them in my car."

"Then it seems to me, the answer is in your own hands."

Mayer didn't want to hear it. "The amulet represents angels," he said, changing the subject. "How could a man like Hitler ever control angels?"

"If the amulet does possess the power it is said to, whoever holds the amulet wields that power."

"Dandy," Mayer said.

"Why do you think Virginia revealed this to you now, Prometheus?"

Mayer stood, picked up the diary and slid it back into his pocket, then put his lid in place atop his head. "Vera Krupp," he said. He downed the last of the whiskey, thanked the monsignor, and left.

15

MAYER WAS AT Atomic Liquors bright and early the next morning, a pit planted firmly in his gut. When he got there, Cassi was ready and waiting. He'd spent the better part of the night preparing for the expedition, burning poplar to create white ash, then dipping each of his silver bullets into it, before loading the Colt Python he'd recently purchased. He'd also taken the precaution of loading the snub-nosed Chief's Special he kept strapped to his ankle—just in case. It was a habit he'd picked up from Detective Fry.

He'd spend the rest of the evening reviewing what the shaman had told him. When his thoughts weren't centered on the skinwalker, they were on the sigil in his mother's diary, wondering if the amulet really did exist and if there truly was a connection to Vera Krupp. He'd looked at the bundle of letters many times, even held it in his hands, but couldn't quite bring himself to open them—he wasn't ready to hear his mother's voice, even in letters.

Mayer's night had been late and his sleep restless. Not that he should have expected anything else. He did, after all, spend the night in a chair instead of his bed and hadn't even bothered to undress. He rented a small place just to the rear of Atomic Liquors. Virginia had offered it to him some time ago and often allowed him to work off the rent at the bar. It seemed a convenient exchange— that was, until now.

Normally Mayer would have snuck into Joe and Stella's place using the key they had entrusted to him and made himself a cup of Joe to rouse his tired eyes. But the encounter with Virginia was still too fresh, so he'd have to make do without the bean juice. Of course he could've made it in his own apartment, but somehow it just didn't taste the same.

Mayer's plans for the day called for a hike into the escarpment—if the elders permitted—and the clothes he had on from the previous night wouldn't make the grade, so he stripped down and headed for the shower. When he finished, he stepped into a pair of Filson canvas hunting pants and tucked the ends into the horsehide boots he used for hiking. Then he pulled on a long-sleeve, button-up shirt, but decided to forgo the tie. When he was ready to face the world, Mayer donned his lid, picked up the Colt, and stepped outside into the morning darkness, the sun having not yet risen.

Two vehicles were in the parking lot: Mayer's Hornet and Cassi's Fairlane. He got into the Hornet, placed the Colt on the seat next to him, and started the car. Cassi exited her car and walked over to Mayer's. She had on a pair of camel-colored slacks, the bottoms tucked into a pair of lace-up boots that stopped only inches away from her knees, and a white sweater that hugged her body in all the places a sweater should. A brown belt, more decorative than anything, wrapped around her middle, coming to a smart bow in the front. Her cheaters sat atop a multicolored head scarf she had wrapped around her head. A canteen covered in canvas was draped over her shoulder, and her red lips held tight to a Marlboro. She took a last puff, dropped the thing, then ground it out with the toe of her boot, before opening the door and climbing in the front seat.

"Dressed for the part, I see," said Mayer.

"What's wrong with what I'm wearing?" Cassi asked, taking stock of her outfit.

"Nothing, if you're trying for the cover of Cosmo."

"Aw, what do you know?" Cassi said. It was then she noticed the Colt. "Does that have to be here?"

"Afraid of a little iron, Reyes?" Mayer asked.

"No, just the men who wield it," Cassi countered.

Mayer removed his lid and laid it on top of the Colt. "Better?"

"Much," Cassi said sarcastically, then added, "You're in some mood."

"Haven't had my coffee yet."

"Why don't you go inside and get some?"

"No soap," Mayer said and threw the boiler into gear. He headed west to Fifth Street, turned left, took a right onto Charleston, then followed it all the way out to the escarpment. The sun was just beginning to peek over the horizon when Mayer pulled onto the dirt road that led to the trailer. He kept one hand on the steering wheel and placed the other over his hat. Cassi held on to her head scarf. They had bounced about halfway down the road, when they found the group of elders waiting for them.

"I thought *I* was an early riser," Cassi said.

Mayer parked just off the road and got out. He took his lid with him, but left the Colt. Cassi followed as he made his way over to Shaman Mahkah and the other elders of the tribe who were all adorned in ceremonial garb.

"I guess they agreed," Mayer said.

"They did," the shaman confirmed. "With a little persuading. If there truly is a skinwalker up there, the elders of the tribe want to know."

The shaman took Mayer and Cassi to a man with a flowing headdress of feathers, intricate beadwork, and animal fur. He wore a bright red shirt with a beaded breastplate and a neckpiece made of the same beads. Turquoise-encrusted gauntlets protected each wrist. He carried a portion of the wing of an eagle in one hand and a long, beaded pipe in the other.

"This is Chief Gray Eagle," the shaman said. "He will be pronouncing the blessing."

Mayer and Cassi stood as the chief spoke in the language of his ancestors while he waved the wing portion over their heads and around their bodies. The rest of the elders formed a circle around the group. Mayer wasn't sure what the chief said, and the shaman showed no inclination to translate, but he could feel the spirit of the blessing and the protection it offered and he welcomed it.

In truth, Mayer wasn't exactly sure what to expect—possibly rhythmic drumming, perhaps native dances; however, the ceremony seemed to be over before it even started. Words were spoken and blessing pronounced and when it was all over, Mayer thanked the chief and the rest of the elders. "Pesa Mu," he said, knowing that he likely mangled the pronunciation. They didn't seem to mind. Mayer turned to Cassi who was standing next to the shaman. "Shall we go?" he said, and headed back to his Hornet.

Once they all got into the car, Mayer pointed it toward the escarpment and headed down the dirt road.

When they arrived at the trailer, he got out, leaving his lid to cover the Colt, and went to the trunk. The caution tape still covered the stairs leading to the door of the trailer. Mayer took out two pairs of gloves, a flashlight, a shoulder holster, a knife, and a canteen which he had filled the night before. He knew better than to traipse up into the hills outside of Las Vegas without water.

He tossed a pair of gloves to Cassi, then strapped on the holster, slipped the knife into a sheath on the other side of it, and shut the trunk. He returned to the front seat, took the Colt from under his hat, and slid it into place. Then he shut the driver's door, locked the car, pulled the canteen over his shoulder, and put on his cheaters.

"Everyone ready?" he asked.

Like Mayer, the shaman had dressed the part and had brought his own canteen. "Ready," he said.

The two men gave Cassi the once over. "Oh, get over yourselves," she said.

Mayer shook his head, turned, and headed into the hills. The bright blue of a new day was chasing away the last bits of night sky as the sun peeked over the horizon. His thoughts turned to his mother. Sunrises were her favorite. She would wake him at times and the two would sit together and watch mother nature's show. They didn't talk. She would just wrap her arms around him, sometimes in a blanket, and they would watch the sky turn from black to topaz blue, then to orange or pink, before returning again to its natural hue.

The trio headed high up into the escarpment, at first following the trails forged by burros, then climbing over rocks and boulders when there was no trail to follow. At one point they passed a large rock wall replete with petroglyphs carved into the stone by the Paleo-Indians in centuries past. Representations of big horn sheep and other animals native to the area, covered the faces of the rocks, along with signs, symbols, and stick-figure people.

Cassi, despite her choice of clothing and footwear, stayed with the men step for step. They had wandered about an hour, sweat forming on each hiker's brow, when the shaman spotted a cave high above a cliff to their right. "Let's try there," he said.

Mayer agreed and led the way. Had he looked up at this point, he would have noticed an unusually large predatory bird circling overhead.

16

GETTING TO THE cave wasn't as easy as it looked, and it didn't look easy. At one point, when reaching for a better grip, Mayer slipped and fell down a series of unforgiving rocks. He tore his shirt and scraped his side. After Cassi and the shaman helped him back to where he had been, the shaman assessed the damage. He pulled leaves from a nearby bush, wet them with his canteen, and laid them on the wound.

"You'll live," he said.

"That's too bad," Cassi said with a smirk.

Mayer gave her one of his own, then kept climbing.

Cassi was the first to make it over the edge of the cliff—atop Mayer's shoulders—to the entrance of the cave. Mayer and Shaman Mahkah each climbed up the side of the cliff to join her. The cave was large enough for a man to walk upright—so long as he watched his head. Mayer turned on the flashlight and the three entered. They had made it about ten feet in when the shaman stopped them.

"Shine your light down at the ground," he said.

Mayer did as told and found footprints larger than any man could have made. He whistled his surprise. "With feet that big, I'd hate to see the gams on that thing," Mayer said. He was about to take a step when the shaman stopped him.

"No," he said. "You must not step on these."

"Why?" Cassi asked.

"Some skinwalkers can make themselves invisible to the human eye. But even so, it will still leave tracks. If the creature is in front of us, it is very bad to step on a skinwalker's prints. You must step over them," he said. "Like this." The shaman demonstrated, stepping over the tracks with exaggerated movement.

Cassi rolled her eyes.

Mayer made the same movement as the shaman, making sure to step over the prints, not on them.

Cassi huffed, but she did as shown.

They hadn't made it far into the cave when there was suddenly a noticeable change in the air. The damp stillness was replaced by a heaviness that filled Mayer's lungs. He took deep breaths, but was finding it more and more difficult to take in enough air. If he'd been wearing a tie, he would have loosened it. Cassi seemed to be experiencing the same problem. He reached out for her just as an enveloping darkness encompassed them—one that even the flashlight couldn't penetrate.

The shaman stopped, held up his arms, and began to chant. Mayer hoped the man wasn't becoming possessed. He'd performed only one exorcism in his time and wasn't exactly sure he could do it again without help—that is, if he didn't pass out first. As the shaman's chants grew louder, Mayer lost his bearings in the dark and his pulse began to quicken—his breathing shallow, his knees beginning to buckle. It was only when Cassi came up behind him and placed a delicate hand on his back that he was able to recenter himself. He turned, just as Cassi collapsed into his arms.

After what seemed like ages, the darkness began to lift. Mayer had dropped the flashlight when Cassi collapsed. Lying still on the ground, it shone anew. The shaman stopped chanting. He picked up the torch and went over to Mayer.

"Black magic," he said and handed him the flashlight. "A protection spell on the cave."

"A good one at that," Mayer said.

Able to breathe again, Cassi regained her footing, but the color had left her face. Mayer felt almost normal— almost. He took the flashlight from the shaman and lit the walls around them.

It was apparent they were in the right place. Animal skins lined one wall—coyote, cougar, fox—a collection of feathers from different birds below them. Bones, looking very human in nature, were stacked against the opposite wall. Some of them were laid out in a pattern Mayer did not recognize. Almost every bit of the cave was covered in symbols painted on the walls, and just as was the case in the shaman's house, there were various herbs and bottles of colored liquid.

"Don't touch anything," the shaman said, "and be sure not to step on anything that looks like it might be a symbol or a sigil, and do not touch the walls. Those symbols have been made in blood, likely the blood of its victims."

Not far from where they stood, Mayer saw something on the cave floor that caught his attention. A painting made of sand. He flashed his light over it. The sand painting was very intricate, in the style he had seen Native Americans use. Bright colors, seamless blending. It was the painting of a man. A man Mayer recognized immediately. It was R. J. Hawthorne.

Parts of the painting were smeared, as if some type of liquid had been spilled on it. In other places there was what Mayer suspected to be feces. The smell seemed to confirm his suspicions. He called the shaman over.

Cassi came too.

"What do you make of this?" Mayer asked.

"It is a skinwalker all right," the shaman confirmed. "They often make sand paintings of their next victims, then urinate and defecate on the picture."

"That's disgusting!" Cassi proclaimed, her face agreeing with her proclamation. Her color had come back and she was breathing normally.

Mayer moved his light to an adjacent sand painting that had been started, but not finished. This one was of a man as well, and just as with the first one, Mayer recognized him: William James Pierce.

"You know that man?" the shaman asked.

"He's my client," Mayer said.

"Well, he is in a great deal of danger."

Mayer nodded.

"Shh," Cassi said, then cocked her head as if straining to hear. "What's that noise?"

"What noise?" Mayer asked. "I don't hear anything."

Cassi turned to the entrance of the cave. "It's coming from there," she said, arm outstretched.

"I hear it too," the shaman said.

Mayer turned his light on the entrance of the cave. It started as a low rumble, barely audible. But little by little, it grew, until a menacing growl echoed against the cave's walls and seemed to surround them.

"I think we'd better be on our way," the shaman said.

"To where?" Mayer asked. "Whatever that is, it's blocking our only way out."

A set of eyes appeared in the dark in front of them at about knee level. Then another, and another after that. When Mayer shined his light on them, they all turned a glowing yellow. The trio bared their teeth, showing long, yellowish, dripping fangs ready to pierce human flesh.

Coyotes.

17

MAYER DREW HIS weapon and pointed it at the coyotes.

"No!" The shaman called out. "They are under the skinwalker's control. They are not responsible for their actions."

"A lot of good that does us," Mayer said without lowering the gun. "If I shoot above their heads, it might just scare them enough for us to get away."

"That is not a good idea," the Shaman said. "What about ricochet?"

It was a good point—one Mayer should have thought of.

"I will take care of the coyotes," the shaman said. "You two get out."

"We're not leaving without you," Mayer said.

"I will be right behind you. Now go!"

Despite his better judgement, Mayer holstered the Colt, grabbed Cassi's hand, and ran forward, using the flashlight to guide the way. He wasn't sure what the shaman had planned, but hoped the man knew what he was doing. They had just made it to the opening when a large hawk swooped down, talons at the ready. Mayer pushed Cassi out of the way, dropped the flashlight and went for his gun, but couldn't reach it in time. The hawk scraped its talons along Mayer's face, only inches from his eye.

Cassi screamed.

The shaman came rushing out of the cave, just as the hawk was making a turn for a second run. He grabbed the flashlight and shined it into the hawk's eyes. The beam blinded the thing, its eyes turning bright red.

"Run!" the shaman yelled, then took hold of Cassi and jumped to the side of the cliff.

Mayer, on one knee, was about to stand, when a coyote grabbed hold of his trouser leg. He drew his other leg back and sent it flying, connecting with the coyote's snout. It whimpered and let go of his pants. But it had no sooner done so when a second coyote made another attempt.

Mayer swung his canteen, hitting the animal in the head, then scooted backwards on his bottom, pushing with his legs. When he reached the edge of the cliff, he twisted his body and rolled off, landing hard on the rocks below. He laid there on his back for a moment trying to catch his breath. The coyotes looked down at him, then began their slow, determined descent, teeth baring. Mayer forced himself to an upright position, tested his legs, and, finding them fit enough, began an awkward run.

But the coyotes were much faster, and in no time, they had closed in on him. A few more steps and they would have him. Mayer pulled his Colt. It would've been easy to just shoot them, but the shaman wouldn't have approved; however, he said nothing about slowing them down. He turned, took aim, and shot just below the paw of the leading coyote.

The bullet ricocheted off a rock, but the noise and the impact took the coyote by surprise. It misstepped and tumbled to the ground. The coyotes behind it were running far too fast to avoid their leader. They hit it hard and all three tumbled in a great ball.

Mayer, pleased with himself, turned to run. He'd made it only a few steps when the hawk swooped down and scraped its talons across Mayer's back. He would have cried out, but the adrenaline rushing through him masked the pain, so he continued on, as fast as his legs would carry him. He leapt rocks, cacti, and anything else that got in his way as he scrambled down the escarpment, trying hard to keep up with the momentum of his downward progression. He fell several times, and the hawk assaulted him two or three more times—he lost count.

The coyotes had overcome their collision and were quickly catching up.

His shirt was in ribbons and he was bleeding heavily by the time he reached his Hornet, but he made it before the coyotes caught him. Cassi and the shaman were already there.

He ran up to the car and threw his hands on the hood to steady himself. "How did you get here so fast?" he asked, breathless.

"The skinwalker concentrated its efforts on you, ignoring us completely," the shaman said.

Mayer girded his loins, pulled the Colt from his holster, and turned to face the sky.

"It's no use," the shaman said. "The hawk is gone."

"But the coyotes aren't," Cassi said, pointing.

The three animals, breathing almost as heavily as Mayer, had reached the trailer and were closing in.

"Get in," Mayer said. He pointed the gun at the coyotes and slid the keys over the hood to Cassi. She opened the passenger door and dove in—the shaman right behind her. Mayer stepped slowly backward to the driver's side, keeping his gun on the coyotes. They followed—yellow teeth at the ready. He pulled the door open, just as Cassi slammed her hand on the horn. The loud noise startled the beasts, giving Mayer just enough time to jump in and slam the door shut.

He took the keys, started the Hornet, and threw it into gear. Spinning wheels sent dirt flying high as Mayer spun the car around and headed up the road. The coyotes stayed with him for only a few feet before they could no longer keep up with the automobile.

Mayer caught his breath for the first time since the cave. "What in the holy hell was that?" he said to no one in particular.

It was then that something hit the car from the side, strong enough to force Mayer off the road. As the occupants crashed into each other, Mayer quickly recovered and brought the Hornet back in line. Just in time for another hit to the side.

"What is that?" Cassi yelled out.

"The skinwalker," the shaman said matter-of-factly.

"You failed to mention it could outrun a car," Mayer said, just as a loud thud came from above them, then a scraping sound.

"It's on the roof," the shaman said.

"Ya think?" said Mayer.

The Hornet began to shake side-to-side, making it very difficult for Mayer to hold the road. The car's rear end fishtailed repeatedly, and at one point they were on only two wheels.

"He's trying to flip us over," Mayer said. He knew he couldn't keep the car on the road at this pace, and it was clear the skinwalker wasn't going anywhere. He thought for a moment, made a quick decision, then took action. As Mayer rolled down the window, he said to Cassi, "Take the wheel."

"Don't roll down that window!" the shaman called out.

"If I don't do something and do it soon, it's going to flip us." He turned to Cassi. "Mind the pedal," he said and slid himself out the window to a sitting position on the door frame.

"Don't look into its eyes!" The shaman called out.

The skinwalker was indeed on the roof. Its grotesque form hunched over—thick claws gripping into each side of the car. It wasn't quite human, neither was it animal, but instead, a malformed mixture of both human and coyote.

It hadn't yet seen Mayer.

He pulled the Colt from its holster and took aim at the thing's neck. Just as his finger pulled against the trigger, the car hit a bump. The gun fired, but the shot missed by a mile. The skinwalker turned to Mayer with human eyes. It let loose of the car and took a swipe at him with long, sharp claws. Mayer took hold of the door frame and leaned backward—the claws barely missing his face. He came back up quickly, Colt in hand and shot a second time. The skinwalker waved his hand and the bullet dropped, useless, onto the hood. Undaunted, Mayer took aim and shot a third time, but the gun suddenly jammed.

The skinwalker looked at Mayer with a sinister smile.

Mayer tried again, but the Colt wouldn't cooperate.

The skinwalker grabbed the car and rocked it hard to the right, then again to the left. Mayer grabbed hold of the top of the door frame, but as the car jumped to the left, his head slammed hard into the frame. He almost dropped the gun.

Cassi screamed.

Mayer's nose was bleeding. He threw the colt into the back seat and pulled out the Chief's Special. "Any suggestions?" he called out.

"I don't suppose you have any salt?" the shaman asked.

"Glove compartment," Mayer answered.

As the shaman opened the glove compartment, Mayer popped back up with the second gun, and as he pointed it at the skinwalker, he was met with the business end of a blowpipe. He saw the projectile coming and pulled his own trigger, just as the tiniest piece of bone fragment lodged itself into Mayer's neck. As he fell backward, he thought he saw the shaman throwing salt at the skinwalker and the creature jump from the hood, high into the air—far higher than any coyote could ever jump. Then Mayer's world went black.

18

WHEN MAYER CAME to he was on the couch, bare chested, in the shaman's home. His neck was throbbing and his back felt like it had been passed over a cheese grater. He reached up to the spot where the pellet had penetrated his skin and found it covered with some type of foul-smelling paste.

"It's a mixture of corn pollen, cedar ash, and juniper berries, along with the gall of a mountain lion," the shaman said. He was holding a cup of steaming liquid. "Drink this."

"Prickly pear?" Mayer asked.

"No, Earl Grey," he said with a smile.

Mayer didn't know what the gall of a mountain lion was, but he suspected it was likely the source of the smell. When he sat up to take the tea, the room began to spin. He braced himself against the couch.

Diogie growled at him.

"Slowly," the shaman said. "We almost lost you. The poison is still in your system."

Mayer took the cup; the aroma wasn't much better than the paste on his neck. "This isn't Earl Grey," Mayer noted.

"No, but you must drink it all the same."

Mayer took a sip. The acidic taste was strong and sour and reflected on his face.

The shaman chuckled.

Diogie growled.

"I don't suppose you've got a rum chaser?" Mayer asked.

"Better stick with the tea."

Mayer took another sip. It wasn't any better than the first one. "So why isn't my melon splattered all over the road?"

"Your Miss Reyes managed to pull you into the car."

"And still steer the thing?"

"Yes," the shaman said. "People have been known to perform extraordinary feats when the need presents itself."

"I guess so," Mayer said. He brought his hand to his neck. "What hit me?"

The shaman walked to a nearby table of herbs and liquids and produced a small pellet. "We had to cut this out of you," he said, holding the thing between his thumb and finger. "Then we had to treat the poison."

"We?"

"Miss Reyes and I."

Mayer looked around, but it was just the two of them in the room. He hadn't realized that Cassi was not there. "And where is Miss Reyes?"

"She'll be back. I sent her to town to do some research."

"What kind of research?" Mayer asked.

Shaman Mahkah moved a chair over to Mayer. "I called and spoke with a Navajo elder about our little situation," he said. "He knew a bit more about the skinwalker and once I was able to confirm its presence, he was willing to tell me what he knew."

Mayer noted the shaman had changed the subject, but let it pass. "Great," he said. "Did he tell you how to kill something that can run faster than a car, stop bullets in mid-air, and make guns jam?"

"Actually, he did. He said that if you can get it to talk to you in its animal form, then it will turn back into a human and be unable to transform ever again. That, however, will not stop it from seeking its revenge upon you and since it will still be able to perform black magic, it doesn't seem like much of an option. There is, perhaps, one better."

"I'm listening," Mayer said.

"You can call it by its real name," the shaman said. "But you must say it's full name, followed by 'you are a skinwalker.'"

"And that will kill it?" Mayer asked, suspiciously. "All I have to do is say 'you are a skinwalker,' and it will just up and die?"

"You must call it by its real name first, but, yes, after a period of three days, it will become sick and die as a result of the wrong it has committed."

"And how am I supposed to find out its real name?"

"That is what Miss Reyes is researching."

"I think we've gotten her involved enough in this whole thing."

"That may be true, but skinwalkers are able to live much longer than you or I. There is no telling how long this creature has been walking the earth. You will have to do much research, and it seems to me it would be quite handy to have someone on your side who is adept at such things. Besides, didn't Theodosia explain that you needed the help of others?"

Mayer stared at the shaman for a moment, wondering how the man knew what Theodosia had said to him—especially since she wasn't one to talk out of school. But the shaman was right and so was Theo, so he left it alone.

"There's one thing I don't get," Mayer said. "If the skinwalker is a Navajo, what is it doing on Paiute land?"

"That is a good question, but one for which I have no answer."

"Well maybe you'll have better luck with this one. Why would the skinwalker make Hawthorne sign over his part of the project to a person who was thwarting him every step of the way?"

"That one's easy," the shaman said. "Skinwalkers are pranksters. They like to play with people's lives, cause as many problems as they can."

Mayer wasn't sure he bought that. Not that he didn't believe that the skinwalker wouldn't cause trouble wherever it could, it just seemed too much of a coincidence that a Native American—even a skinwalker—made a man sign over his portion of a project that would defile sacred land to a woman who seemed bent on protecting that very land. The bigger question to Mayer was why a Navajo would care about land sacred to Paiutes.

"Could a Paiute become a skinwalker?" Mayer asked.

"I suppose it is possible," the shaman said. "But not likely. It is against everything we stand for. Everything that is Paiute. That said, it has been my experience that evil exists everywhere and in all forms. I suppose that if a Navajo could go against his beliefs and become a skinwalker, I imagine a Paiute could as well."

Mayer finished the liquid and placed the cup down on the table next to the couch. "I don't suppose you have a shirt I could borrow?" he asked.

The shaman seemed to know what was coming next. "You are in no condition to leave, and in even less condition to drive."

"Nix that," Mayer said. He scooted himself to the edge of the couch and made an attempt to stand. It didn't take, but it didn't stop him. On his second try, he was able to get his legs under him and, after the room stopped spinning, he took a step and then another. His legs were noodles and his back was a lesson in pain, but he had a job to do, so he pressed on.

The shaman shook his head, said something in Paiute and left the room. He came back with a turquoise blue pullover shirt and handed it to Mayer.

Mayer eyed it cautiously. "This all you got?"

"I believe the phrase is beggars cannot be choosers."

The shaman had a point, so Mayer slipped his arms into the shirt and pulled it over his head. He would have groaned with the pain it caused, but didn't want to hear it from his makeshift doctor. "I'll get this back to you," he said.

"Keep it. Call it a souvenir."

Mayer thanked him, picked up his effects from the table by the couch where the shaman had placed them, and headed for the door.

"Do not go after the skinwalker alone," the shaman said. "Its magic is far too powerful. Had I not been there, you would still be in that cave. This is better handled by the elders."

Mayer nodded, but he didn't intend to listen. He now knew where the skinwalker could be found and what he needed to do. Before he stepped out the door, he turned to the shaman. "Will you be okay out here all by yourself?"

"I am not ever by myself," the shaman said. "I have my ancestors and Diogie. I will be all right."

"But the skinwalker knows about you now."

"Even a skinwalker cannot enter a house uninvited, and I have no intention of inviting it in."

Mayer nodded.

"If you insist on going up there by yourself, you must take this." The shaman handed Mayer a small brown bottle.

"What is it?"

"The gall of a mountain lion. Use it if the witch blows corpse powder at you or hits you with another bone pellet. Of course, you'll probably die before you can use it effectively."

"Great, thanks," Mayer said blandly.

As Mayer stepped out the door, the shaman said, "No one will think less of you if you change your mind, Mr. Mayer. It would be better to make a plan, better yet to let the elders handle this."

Mayer waved the shaman off. When he got to his Hornet, he assessed the damaged. Scratches marred the roof, down through the paint to the metal. He walked over to the passenger's side; it was dented from the impact. *There goes the five hundred*, he said to himself. It was then that he noticed a substance on the roof, like blood, only yellow. Perhaps he had hit the beast after all. He went to the driver's side, climbed in, and started the car. He had a stop to make before he went back into the hills.

GOING AFTER THE skinwalker alone was a foolish thing to do, but the shaman could see that Mayer was set to the task and nothing would dissuade him. He shut the door and sighed heavily. Diogie pawed his leg.

"I suppose you are right, Diogie. Even Mr. Mayer deserves help, as stubborn as he is. Without me, he will likely die."

The shaman changed his clothes, laid out food for Diogie, and prepared a satchel with the herbs and tokens he would need to face off against the creature. He adorned himself with protective jewelry around his neck and wrists and put on the chest plate made of maize. He hadn't worn any of it when he went up with Mayer and that had been a mistake, but, then again, he didn't really believe they would find a skinwalker; he was just appeasing Mayer for Theodosia. He knew better now. Taking a ceremonial staff, one decorated with eagle feathers and tobacco leaves, he headed for the door.

"You must stay here and guard the house, Diogie. I will be back after a while."

He took a salt container and spread a line against the door's threshold, just in case.

Diogie began to growl. The hair raising on the ridge of his back.

"It is okay, Diogie. I will be fine."

Diogie barked his disapproval.

The shaman opened the door and was about to step out when a powder was blown directly in his face. He looked ahead and saw a creature, more animal than human, the palm of the hand outstretched in front of the thing's mouth—one which formed an unholy smile.

The shaman tried not to inhale, but it was too late. He started to choke as his throat began to swell. The room was spinning. He could hear Diogie barking and thought he saw him leap for the door. It was the last thing he would see before he hit the ground.

19

MAYER NEEDED A change of clothes so he headed to his apartment behind Atomic Liquors. The parking lot behind the tavern was filled with vehicles from the lunchtime crowd. Mayer noticed Cassi's Fairlane was not among them. At just about the same time Mayer climbed out of the car, Joe Sobchick came out the back door of the bar, carrying a large bag of trash.

"Well there you are," he said to Mayer.

"Here I am," Mayer said back.

Joe threw the garbage into the bin and stepped closer to Mayer. "What the heck are you wearing? And what happened to your face?"

"Some palooka took exception to what I said about his skirt," Mayer said.

"Must have pawed you pretty good." Joe said, then looking at the Hornet, asked, "Did your car insult her too?"

"Something like that."

"Stella's looking for you. She's inside," he said, making a motion with his thumb.

"Dandy."

Joe softened his face. "I heard what happened with Virginia," he said.

"That why Stella wants to see me?"

Joe nodded. "That and a Detective Fry has been trying to get ahold of you."

"Virginia inside?" Mayer asked.

"No. Haven't seen her all day."

"Tell Stella I'll be there in a bit. I need to freshen up first."

Joe nodded and headed inside. Mayer went to the trunk of his Hornet and put everything back in its proper place, including the canteen and the Colt he retrieved from the floor of the back seat where each had landed. When he was done, he shut the trunk and went to his apartment.

He stepped over the threshold of salt, and flicked on the light. Everything seemed to be in order, so he headed for the bedroom, stripped down, and went for a shower. He turned on the hot water faucet and left the cold one alone. When there was enough steam for a Turkish bath, he pulled the curtain and stepped inside. He stood there, allowing the hot water to bring him back to life. After a while he tried soap. It stung at first, but he wasn't afraid of pain. Lots of things in life hurt. Mayer had learned to live with them.

Once he had cleansed himself of the evil, he turned off the water, wrapped the towel around his waist, then stepped from the shower to the porcelain sink. He wiped the steam from the mirror on the medicine cabinet and had a look. The talons had just missed his eye and the marks were already turning a bright red.

Perfect.

He decided a shave was in order—not remembering the last time he'd performed the task—so he opened the medicine cabinet and removed his brush, cream, and razor. He lathered up, then scraped the whiskers from his face and chin, only nicking himself twice in the process. It added to the veneer.

He found a clean pair of trousers, a long-sleeve, button-down Nubby shirt, socks, and the boots he wore to the cave. He slid a belt around his waist, got his cheaters, and readied himself for Stella. He was about to leave when he remembered the small brown bottle the shaman had given him. While filling his canteen, he decided a bit of rum was in order. In the kitchenette he found a small, brown bottle of Black Heart Demerara and poured two fingers into a glass. He did it twice more before heading out the door to Atomic Liquors.

When he entered the place, Stella was tending bar, making a horse's neck, by spiraling an entire lemon with a paring knife. She slid the lemon into a Collins glass, filled it with ice, added a jigger of whiskey, and filled the rest with ginger ale. It was a nasty drink that only nasty people drank.

She saw Mayer and motioned him over to the bar. "Well, look what the cat drug in," she said. "You look like hell in a handbasket."

Mayer couldn't argue the point. "I feel even worse," he said.

"Fry's been trying to get ahold of you. Called here three times already."

Mayer slipped behind the bar, picked up the blower, and dialed. When the desk sergeant answered, he asked to be connected to Detective Fry.

"Fry here," the detective said.

"I hear you're looking for me."

"Bout time you showed."

"I was detained."

"Yeah, well, I thought you might like to know that your body's gone."

"Excuse me?"

"Your body at the morgue, it's gone."

"You mean Hawthorne?"

"Yeah, Hawthorne. He's gone."

"What do you mean he's gone? Did someone claim his body?"

"Couldn't," Fry said. "There's nothing to claim. He's gone, vanished, vamoosed, hasta la vista."

"What happened?"

"Officially? No one knows. Unofficially, got a call from my guy down at the morgue. Told me the drawer opened, Hawthorne climbed out, then he up and left."

"And no one stopped him?"

"What was there to stop? First of all, the guy's a stiff. Second, if a dead guy doesn't want to hang around, who are we to stop him? I figured this is your area. Find anything out yet?"

"Couple things."

"You need my help?"

"Not yet. I'll let you know if I do," Mayer said and hung up.

Stella gave Mayer a disapproving look—something she'd learned from her mother. "What did you do?" she asked.

"I don't have the slightest idea what you're talking about," Mayer said. "You have any coffee?"

Stella pointed to a pot. "Just brewed," she said.

Mayer found a cup and poured himself the first coffee of the day. He slipped back around the bar and took one of the stools. Atomic Liquors was full of people who stopped in for a quick snort on their way home from work or on their way to work from home. Mayer sipped his coffee while Stella tended customers.

The phone rang.

"Wanna get that?" Stella said, busy with customers.

Mayer took another sip of Joe, then walked around the bar and picked up the receiver.

"Atomic Liquors. Home of the atomic cocktail."

"Mayer, is that you?" the female voice asked with breathless anticipation.

"Yeah, it's me."

"It's Cassi," she said. "I'm at the shaman's house."

"Yeah, sorry about that, I . . ."

She cut him off. "I think he's dead!"

"What?"

"He's lying on the floor; his tongue is black and it doesn't look like he's breathing." Panic was rising in her voice. "I found Diogie in the yard, his side slashed. What should I do?"

"Did you call an ambulance?"

"Yes, but I don't think he can wait. What should I do?" she asked a second time.

Mayer thought for a minute, then remembered the small bottle in his pocket. He pulled it out, took a glass from the shelf and poured a little inside. The greenish liquid was putrid. Stella flashed him another of her looks.

"Go to his shelf of herbs and liquids," Mayer said to Cassi. "Look for a brown bottle, possibly small."

"Okay," she said, her nervousness coming soundly across the phone.

"You're looking for a greenish liquid with a horrid odor. Go for the smell first, then try the color."

"I'll have to put the phone down," she said.

"Just do it!"

Mayer sat in silence while Cassi, he presumed, did as instructed. The scenery blurred like the background in a photograph and the sounds of the bar seemed to drift away. All Mayer could hear was a slight beating he assumed was his heart—or maybe it was Cassi's. Seconds passed like hours as he waited . . . and waited.

Cassi's voice finally came back on the phone. "I think I found it," she said, but she didn't sound sure.

"Does it smell?" Mayer asked.

"Yes, horribly."

"And is it green?"

"Greenish," she confirmed.

"You need to pour that into the shaman's mouth," Mayer said.

"Can't you just . . ."

"There isn't time," Mayer said. "Just do it, Reyes!"

"I don't . . ."

Mayer could hear the panic growing in her voice. He changed tactics. "Cassi," he said in a softer tone. "You're the only one who can help him now. I have faith in you. Just take the bottle over to the shaman, pour a little on his lips and down his throat. Don't do too much or he will choke. Just a little, now. Go ahead. Put the phone down and go on."

"Okay," Cassi said.

Mayer did his best to listen through the phone line. He could hear Cassi breathing and what sounded like a dog bark. Then, after a long silence, he heard a cough and a sputter, followed by another.

"He's coming to," Cassi said loudly.

"Atta Girl!" Mayer said, but he knew she couldn't hear him.

20

MAYER STAYED ON the phone with Cassi until the ambulance showed. The shaman had regained his voice before they arrived and told Cassi how to contact the elders for help. He also guided her to mix herbs into a liquid that he could drink, then he helped her create a paste to put on Diogie's wounds.

Cassi related the events to Mayer, explaining that the shaman told her it had been the skinwalker who had attacked him and that he suspected the witch blew corpse powder in his face. She said he also wanted to thank Mayer for his quick action, and thanked her as well.

After Mayer hung up, he immediately made another call. This one to William James Pierce. "I've got an update," he told him. "It's urgent I speak to you."

"I'm glad you called," Pierce said. "I have news for you as well. Can you come to my home?"

Mayer said he could, then wrote the directions down on a cocktail napkin. Stella tried to stop him before he left. "We need to talk," she said, but Mayer told her it would have to wait for another time. He jumped into what was left of his Hornet and followed the directions Pierce had given him. He was at the man's home in less than fifteen minutes.

Pierce lived in a part of town known as the Scotch 80s. His house, a modest 3,000-square-foot ranch, was on Bannie Avenue off of Pine Street. Mayer parked in the circular driveway, slipped on his lid, and got out of the car. He was about to knock on the door, then he thought it might be best to go in heavy. It wasn't Pierce he was worried about, but the creature, so he popped the trunk and donned his shoulder holster, a freshly loaded Colt, and a knife with a silver blade. He also grabbed a large container of salt. If what Mayer saw in the cave was any indication of things to come, Pierce was going to need it.

He closed the trunk and rang the doorbell. Pierce's man opened the door, eyed Mayer's Colt, and put his hand to Mayer's chest. "I'll need that rod." he said.

"I like it right where it is," Mayer countered.

"Let him in," Pierce called out from the next room.

Pierce's man removed his hand and motioned with his head for Mayer to go in, but kept a wary eye on him.

The expansive house had a very open floor plan with the kitchen, living room, sitting room, bar, dining room, and pool table on the first floor. Pierce was in what passed for a living room, one large enough to fit Mayer's entire apartment—and probably Atomic Liquors as well. A velvet evening jacket with black lapels covered his white shirt and tie. He had a dead pipe in his hand and was wearing down the carpet in front of a fireplace. He turned when Mayer entered the room, his eyes wide.

"It that really necessary?" he asked. "My man can handle anything that would require firearms."

"Really?" asked Mayer. "Does your Bruno carry silver bullets?"

Pierce furrowed his brow. "Why on earth would a man carry silver bullets?" he asked.

"Because lead won't cut it."

"I'm sure I don't know what you're talking about," Pierce said.

Mayer stepped into the large room and took a seat in a black leather chair with studded arms. He crossed one leg over the other, then set the salt down on the end table next to the chair. Pierce's man moved to a corner of the room behind him.

"Is your man particular to that corner, or can you have him stand in another?" Mayer asked. "I get jumpy with birds behind me."

Pierce motioned for the man to move, which he did begrudgingly. "What happened to your face?" Pierce asked.

"Cut myself shaving."

Pierce formed a disapproving frown. "What have you to tell me?" he asked.

"Perhaps you ought to go first," Mayer countered.

"Vera Krupp came to see me today."

"Did she now?"

"It is her intention to stop the project entirely. She is going to donate her newly inherited portion to the Paiute Tribal Council."

"And that's a bad thing?" Mayer asked.

"Of course it's a bad thing," Pierce said with a glare. "Not only will it kill the project, it will ruin me. I've invested more than a hundred thousand dollars into this project, all to have that idiot Hawthorne screw it up."

It was quite a way to speak of the dead, Mayer thought, but then again, he knew that money makes people say foolish things. "It's not entirely his fault," Mayer offered.

"Oh? Isn't it?" Pierce said sharply. "I warned him. I told him not to get involved with . . ."

Pierce stopped; his breath, suddenly visible, trailed off in front of him. The sight unsettled him and it showed. The air inside grew cold and the lights began to flicker, catching both Pierce's and Mayer's attention. An animal of some kind howled outside, followed by long harrowing scratches along the side of the house and across the glass. Pierce seemed to catch movement out the window.

"Go check that out," Pierce ordered his man.

Mayer jumped from his chair. "Nix that!" he ordered. "Don't open that door."

The hired man pulled his gun from his own shoulder holster and held it up by his head. "I can handle anything stupid enough to be out there," he said.

"Don't be a bunny," Mayer countered. He picked up the salt and headed to the front door.

"What are you doing?" Pierce asked.

"What you hired me for." Mayer spread a line of salt next to the threshold. "How many doors you got to this place that lead out?" he asked.

Pierce stumbled on his words. "I don't know, three or four."

The scratching grew louder.

"Cheese that cannon and get busy spreading this salt in front of each door," Mayer said and threw the salt to Pierce's hired man. He caught it clumsily. "Do it just as I did here, end-to-end in one long stream. Don't leave any breaks."

The hired man didn't move.

"Do it!" Mayer yelled.

Pierce motioned for his man to do as told.

"I don't understand . . ."

Mayer cut Pierce off. "I don't have time to explain," he said. "Just do as I tell you."

"William James Pierce," a macabre, haunting voice called from outside. "You have betrayed me, William. Now come out and play."

Pierce's face lost all its color. "It can't be," he said. "It just can't be."

Mayer was confused. "You know that voice?" he asked.

"Yes," Pierce said quickly, his eyes wide as saucers. "But it can't be. It just can't be!"

"Who?" Mayer asked. "Who can't it be?"

"Hawthorne," Pierce said. "That's R. J. Hawthorne's voice!"

He no sooner said it than a vapor of the man appeared directly in front of them. Hawthorne was in death just as he had been in life, at least at the end of his life, with a large portion of the left side of his head missing—a gunshot wound on the right side. His eyes vacant. He seemed to be pointing at Pierce, but it wasn't a real point because the ghost was missing a forefinger.

The lights flickered.

"You betrayed me," the voice said, but it wasn't coming from the ghost. It, like the scratching, was coming from outside the house, surrounding it in a ghostly echo. "I know what you did, William, and I know why you did it."

That fact seemed lost on Pierce who was fixated by his dead partner. "It can't be you," Pierce said, incredulously. "You're dead!"

"Very," Hawthorne's voice said. "Thanks to you."

Mayer slipped closer to the fireplace. Though Hawthorne's voice was ringing through the walls of Pierce's home, it definitely wasn't coming from Hawthorne's ghost, which begged the question, *where was it coming from?* Mayer wasn't sure he wanted the answer.

The spirit stepped closer to Pierce and Pierce closer to Mayer, just as Pierce's hired man came back into the room. "I'm . . . holy . . ." he blurted out, dropping the salt in front of him. Hawthorne turned, and swiping his hand from right to left, flung the man's body into the wall by the door.

Mayer seized upon the moment. He grabbed the iron poker next to the fireplace and attacked the ghost. It disappeared, then reappeared at Mayer's side, but Mayer expected it and kept swinging the iron, passing it through Hawthorne, until the spirit, weakened by the iron, could no longer manifest. Then he ran to the salt, scooped it up, and returned to Pierce. He made a circle with the salt and instructed Pierce to remain in that circle.

"Take this," Mayer said, handing the poker to Pierce. "Ghosts don't do well with iron."

Mayer looked to Pierce 's man, who was just getting back on his feet. "You better get over here too," he said.

At just that moment, something came crashing through the living room window on the left, sending shards of glass in all directions. Something more beast than man, more coyote than human. Something Mayer had just seen that very morning.

"My god, what is that?" Pierce asked, his eyes saucers.

"A skinwalker," Mayer said, his voice rising. "Stay in the circle and don't look it in the eyes!"

The skinwalker rose from its crouched position, rising high above both Mayer and Pierce. Pierce took a step backward. The creature positioned itself, directly in front of the two men and as the light of a nearby lamp caught his eyes, they turned flame red.

"What the hell is a . . ."

Before Mayer's client could finish his sentence, Hawthorne's ghost reappeared and took hold of Pierce by the shoulders, lifting him high off the ground. Pierce dropped the poker.

"How the . . ." Mayer said, then noticed the salt circle had been broken, likely when the skinwalker came crashing through the window.

Pierce's mouth dropped agape. Dark veins began to appear on his neck and he started making gurgling noises. At the same time, Pierce's hatchet man rose and, standing behind the creature, took aim with a shaky hand. Mayer called out to stop him, but it was too late, the man began emptying his heater at the creature. Some of the bullets hit the thing, most did not. Mayer ducked as stray pills shot across the room. Some embedded into the wall behind him. Others crashed into chairs and vases, destroying items that cost more than Mayer would make in a year. One cut through Pierce's shoulder.

"Stop shooting!" Mayer cried out.

The creature turned on Pierce's man. It leapt to him in one swift movement, landing directly on top of his chest. Before he could even cry out, the creature had torn out his throat. While keeping an eye on the skinwalker,

Mayer stepped closer to Pierce, who was now firmly in the grip of Hawthorne's ghost. His experience in the car and how quickly the creature could move was fresh in his mind. Still, he knew that if he didn't do something quickly, Pierce would be joining his partner on the other side. His eyes had already rolled into the back of his head and the dark veins on his neck had overtaken his face as well. His body limp.

Mayer bent down and took hold of the dropped poker. He was about to swing it at the ghost, when the skinwalker turned to Pierce and Mayer. It began a slow but determined walk toward them. Mayer drew the Colt from his holster with his left hand—thankful he'd been taught to shoot with both equally as well. Something drilled into him when he was first learning to shoot. "What if you can't use your right?" the instructor had asked him. "Then what will you do?" Mayer thought it an inconvenience at the time, but was now thankful he'd listened.

"Wanna have a go at mine?" he asked.

As the skinwalker approached, Mayer took a tentative poke at the ghost with no effect. He stepped closer to Pierce, and as he did, he kicked up a portion of the salt from the floor at the ghost. The act weakened the ghost, causing it to flicker, and as it did, Mayer took a mighty swing with the poker. As he had hoped, the combination of the two broke the specter's grip on Pierce; his body falling hard to the floor.

Mayer positioned himself between Pierce and his two opponents—poker in one hand and Colt in the other, the fireplace to his rear. He turned his attention back to the skinwalker. The creature was blocking their only method of escape, and even if they could make it out the door, little good it would do against something that could outrun a car. It was still coming toward him, but taking its time to do so. Its gruesome face formed a smile; almost as if it was enjoying the show.

Mayer kept his Colt in position and wondered how he was to aim at the creature's neck without looking into its eyes. As the creature continued its approach, Mayer noticed something he hadn't seen before. There was already a wound at the creature's neck. A fresh nick with what looked like a dried yellow liquid.

Mayer smiled. "Guess I got you last time, didn't I?" he said.

The creature stopped and placed a clawed hand at its neck, then looked back at Mayer with raging eyes. Once again moving forward. Mayer made sure not to look into those eyes for too long, keeping the Colt in position. He didn't think it would work, but he was willing to try what the elder had told Shaman Mahkah. If he could get the creature to talk, he might have a better chance to take it out.

"Afraid I might be a better shot this time?" he asked. "Or maybe you're just not as bad as you think you are. You can't get Pierce and you couldn't get the shaman."

The skinwalker stopped.

"Oh, you didn't know?" Mayer asked. "Your little corpse powder trick didn't work. The shaman is alive and well."

The creature's mouth began to form words, just as Pierce cried out from behind Mayer. "What are you doing? Shoot the thing!"

The creature glanced quickly down at Pierce and then back at Mayer, who pulled the trigger, but nothing happened. He pulled it two more times with the same result.

Hawthorne flickered back into the room.

"Do something!" Pierce yelled.

Mayer threw the poker down at Pierce, reasoning that if he was alive, then he could darn well help. Then he switched the gun into his right hand, drew the knife from its sheath with his left, and readied himself for battle. He watched the skinwalker from the corner of his eye, until he too heard a voice from his past. A soft voice. A caring voice. A mother's voice.

"Prometheus," it said. "Why are you doing this? Why are you wasting your life chasing ghosts?"

Mayer turned his full attention to the skinwalker. "Mother?" he asked, unsure, at first, where the voice originated. He watched as the creature finished its transformation right in front of him. Its fangs receded. Its ears rounded and moved down to the sides of its head. Standing erect on legs now more human than animal, it was somehow smaller, shorter than before, with a distinctly female face—one with the eyes of an animal. The woman in front of him was now naked, except for the coyote skins covering her back and head and the multiple markings and symbols decorating her painted body.

"Yes, Prometheus," the witch said. "It's time to stop this nonsense. Time to come home."

Mayer lowered the knife and the Colt as well. "Mother?" he asked a second time.

"Time to come home, Prometheus."

Tears were forming in Mayer's eyes. He hadn't read the letters, not wanting to hear his mother's voice, even in his head. Not wanting to deal with the pain of losing her once again. But her voice had found him and the pain had come anyway.

"Go ahead, son. Take the gun and move it to your head. Then you can come home."

The house and everything in it drifted away. Pierce was gone, Hawthorne had disappeared. All that was left was Mayer and the woman standing in front of him... and the Colt Python he had just purchased. A .357, double-action, magnum revolver, with a full barrel underlug, ventilated rib, and adjustable sights. He'd chosen the six-inch barrel over the four-and-a-quarter-inch to give it better velocity and less recoil, but also for the balance.

He stared at the gun.

"That's right," his mother said. "Now cock the hammer."

Mayer placed his thumb on the hammer and pulled it back until it clicked. The cylinder turned, positioning one silver bullet into the barrel, ready for projection once the hammer was released.

"Good. Now bring it to your head."

Mayer didn't want to bring the gun to his head, but he hadn't wanted to cock the hammer either and yet he did. He did because his mother told him to, because the voice was all he could hear. Now his mother wanted him to bring the Colt to his head, so he did. He raised his arm and positioned the gun against his temple, his finger firmly on the trigger, and as he did, his sleeve slid back slightly, as sleeves tend to do when arms are raised, revealing his Helm of Awe tattoo.

The female form in front of Mayer froze, and as it did, the haze occupying Mayer's mind began to lift. The darkness surrounding him lifted as well and the room came back. Mayer removed the gun from the side of his head and stared at it as if it was some foreign object. He could hear a voice calling out to him—yelling at him. "Shoot!" it said. "Shoot the thing!"

Mayer turned his head to the source of the voice. It was Pierce, now standing, yelling at him and clutching his shoulder.

He turned back to the skinwalker. The creature cried out a piercing scream, then transformed a second time, back into the animal it once was. Grey and brown fur covered the body. Pointed ears sat atop an animal's head. Yellow fangs reappeared where teeth had once been, along with eyes more human than animal. Eyes, that for the first time since Mayer had first seen them, showed fear. The creature took one last look, then leapt back through the same window it had used to come in, just as Mayer raised the Colt and pulled the trigger.

21

MAYER STOOD STARING at the tattoo on his wrist. He wasn't quite sure what had happened, but he understood one thing. The tattoo had frightened the creature enough to make it leave. It had also shocked the thing into releasing Mayer from its spell. He took the opportunity to shoot at it on its way out, though he doubt he hit anything. The skinwalker had gone away for now, but there was still one more issue to deal with.

Hawthorne.

He was standing there, flashing in and out like a television with bad reception. Mayer holstered the Colt, snatched the poker, stepped over what was left of the salt circle, and began swinging it at Hawthorne. Hawthorne tried once more, but didn't have enough spiritual energy to fully materialize. Mayer easily dispatched the apparition with a halfhearted swipe.

He went over to the telephone, dropped the poker on the chair, then picked up the receiver and dialed.

"Who are you calling?" Pierce questioned.

"The police," Mayer said.

Pierce took a step forward, then stopped when he realized he was at the edge of the circle. "Please," he pleaded. "No police."

Mayer held a palm up toward Pierce. "Don't worry," he assured him. "I know who to call."

After the line connected, Mayer, once again asked for Detective Fry. When the detective answered, Mayer said, "Found Hawthorne, well, sort of."

"Great," said Fry. "You find a hole in the ground to put him in?"

"Not quite. But I could use some of that help you offered earlier. I've got a bit of a situation here."

Fry sighed. "Give me the address."

Mayer did as requested and suggested the detective come alone. When he was finished, he hung up and glanced over at Pierce. Concern wrinkled the man's forehead and embedded itself in the lines around his eyes.

"You don't need to stay in that circle now," Mayer said.

Pierce remained in position, clutching his arm.

Mayer went to him. "Let's get your fancy jacket off and have a look at that arm," he said.

Pierce nodded but didn't move his hand, so Mayer did it for him. He slid the coat from the man's shoulder, pulling it downward and off. Then he tossed it onto a nearby chair. The sleeve of Pierce's shirt was stained with his own blood, a small tear at the top. Mayer grabbed hold of the shirt on either side of the tear and pulled, ripping the opening even wider. Pierce winced. The bullet had not entered his shoulder. It had only nicked the skin and the wound had already stopped bleeding.

But it was clear Pierce was in shock, if not due to the near miss, then to the attack itself. Mayer went to Pierce's bar and poured him a snort in a short glass. "Here," he said, handing it to Pierce. "Better nibble one."

When Pierce hesitated, Mayer pushed the glass into his hand. "Drink it," he ordered.

Pierce looked distantly at the glass, then wrapped his fingers around it, before bringing it to his mouth, and slamming it down in one try.

"Whoa, there," Mayer cautioned. "Slow down with that." He took the glass, refilled it, and handed it back to Pierce.

Pierce nodded slowly. His eyes were beginning to come back from the saucers they had turned into and the color was returning to his face. He loosened his tie and undid his top button, then he took another drink, sipping it this time. "What on earth was that?" he asked.

"That was the thing that killed your partner," Mayer said. "The thing that's coming for you as well."

"For me?" Pierce asked, incredulously. "Why would it be coming for me?"

"Well that's the question, isn't it?" Mayer said. He took the poker from the chair and returned it to the fireplace. "But what I don't get is how it was able to come into the house?"

Pierce looked confused.

"It has to be invited," Mayer said. "It can't just come in on its own."

"Well, I certainly did not invite it in."

"You must have. This is your house." He looked over at the dead man lying by the door—the pool of blood around his neck. "Unless your hired man did it for you."

"I don't see how he could have."

Mayer rubbed his hands together—a habit of his father's he'd picked up when he was trying to think—and walked over to the open window. "Who's come to your house lately?" he asked Pierce.

"No one to speak of," Pierce answered. "Gardeners, the housekeeper, the cook last evening."

Mayer watched Pierce's eyes, for they were the key to the soul. He knew that if a man lied, it would show there. "And Vera Krupp," he added.

"Yes. Vera Krupp," Pierce confirmed.

"Tell me about that."

"What's there to tell?" Pierce asked. He picked up his smoking jacket and examined the tear in the shoulder—one matching the tear in his shirt. He reached into the inner pocket and removed a fancy silver cigarette case, the same one he'd had in the bar. He opened it, took out a single slim, brown cigarette, and slid an end into his mouth.

"She came to tell me she intended to donate her portion of the project to the Paiute Tribal Council," Pierce continued, the cigarette bouncing as he spoke. He reached into the outside pocket of the jacket and produced a chrome Ronson cigarette lighter with the initials W. J. P. inscribed in a plate on the side. He pressed the lever with a shaky finger, produced a flame, and chased the end of the cigarette.

"Why would she come all the way over here just to tell you that?" Mayer asked.

"You'd have to ask her," Pierce said, taking a quick drag. "Perhaps she wanted to rub it in. Wanted to see my face as she pronounced my ruin." He took another drag, then said, "The kraut."

That didn't sit well with Mayer. It didn't make sense, and he had learned long ago not to trust things that didn't make sense—they typically aren't true. He was about to push it when a knock came at the door. Pierce moved to answer, but Mayer stopped him. "Better let me do it," he said.

"Who is it?" Mayer asked.

"Who do you think it is?" the voice said from the other side of the door.

Mayer opened the door slowly and poked his head around the side. He figured it was Fry, seeing as the skinwalker didn't show a propensity to knock, but he wanted to make sure just the same. Fry pushed the door open with his palm, almost hitting Mayer in the process.

"What've ya got?" he asked, then let out a long, slow whistle when he saw the body spread out on the floor. "He looks worse than you," Fry said to Mayer motioning to his face, then asked, "This your doing?"

"Not quite," said Mayer.

Fry crouched down and examined the body. He looked up at Mayer with a suspicious eye. "What am I supposed to do with this?"

"I was hoping you could tell me."

Fry stood and had a look around the room. He motioned to Pierce with his thumb. "Who's he?"

"William James Pierce," Mayer said. "He owns the place."

"That his man?"

Mayer nodded.

Fry addressed Pierce. "Why do you need a gunsel?"

"I assure you, Officer, Mr. Harding was no gunsel. His scruples were beyond reproach."

"For the right price, you mean," Fry said. "And it's Detective."

"My apologies, Detective. I meant no offense."

"Forget it," Fry said. "But you didn't answer my question."

"Not everyone is in favor of the project I am currently undertaking. Some people have objected, rather strongly. Mr. Harding was here for personal protection."

Mayer watched as Fry gave the room the once over, his detective eye not missing a single bit of evidence—not one bullet hole or broken vase. Fry removed his lid and scratched his head at the bald spot in the back with the same hand. He rubbed the other across his stubbled chin.

"Looks like a rabid coyote jumped through that window," he said, pointing with hatted hand. "Then your Mr. Harding started shooting, without hitting anything—except for Pierce, of course," he said inclining his head to Pierce. "And then it attacked Harding, tearing out his pipes, before leaving the way it came in. Sound about right?"

"Sounds good to me," Mayer said.

"Good. Now why don't you tell me what really happened."

22

FRY WANTED TO have a look at the front of the house, so he stepped outside. Mayer followed. When the two were along, Mayer told Fry everything that had happened, including his visit with the shaman and their trip to the skinwalker's cave. He ended with the events at Pierce's house, the appearance of Hawthorne's ghost and the skinwalker crashing through the window.

Fry shook his head slowly. "Boy, when you step in it, you step in it but good. I'll need you both to make a statement. You better clean up that salt, then coach your client on what to say." He paused, then added, "And what not to say."

Within an hour, Pierce's house was swarming with uniforms. Pierce had also managed to get his handyman over to board up the window once the police released the scene. Pierce did as instructed, saying exactly what Mayer had coached him to say the way he'd coached him to say it. The coroner came and removed Harding's body. Fry took his piece.

Mayer made no mention of firing his own Colt to the uniforms, as per Fry's instructions. He'd even removed the gun and holster and placed it in his Hornet, donning his suit coat before they arrived. Pierce was offered medical attention, but declined.

When everyone finally left, taking all their equipment with them, Mayer turned to Pierce. "You can't stay here," he said.

"And why not?" Pierce asked.

Mayer ignored the question, picked up the phone, and dialed. After a moment, the shaman answered. "Feel like a roommate?" Mayer asked.

"It depends entirely on the nature of the roommate."

A grin formed in the corner of Mayer's mouth. "My client, Mr. Pierce. I'm at his home and we've just been attacked by the witch and Pierce's dead partner."

"I see," the shaman said. "Better bring him over then. I can better protect him here."

"Change your clothes and pack an overnight bag," Mayer told Pierce after he hung up the phone. "We'd better leave as soon as possible."

"Where are we going?"

"I'll tell you when we get there," Mayer said.

Twenty minutes later Pierce was ready to leave. He had a clean shirt, a new tie, vest, and sported a double-breasted sack suit, with a matching waistcoat instead of the smoking jacket he had on earlier. In his hand was a small, striped canvas suitcase with red leather trim and a matching handle. A Knox hat was atop his head.

"You didn't have to go all fancy," Mayer said.

Pierce took the measure of his clothes, then said with a raised eyebrow, "I assure you, Mr. Mayer, this is far from *fancy*."

"Do you have anything of Hawthorne's?" Mayer asked. "Anything personal? Anything that might have meant something to him?"

Pierce hesitated.

"Ghosts often attach themselves to items that held importance in their previous lives. If you have such an item, it might allow Hawthorne to keep coming at you. If you want it to stop, I'll need that item."

"And how do you stop it?" Pierce asked.

"Destroy the thing," Mayer said bluntly.

Pierce brought his hand absentmindedly to his suit coat where the inside pocket would be. "I don't believe I have such an object," he said. But he had no sooner finished when Mayer went to him, pulled the lapel of his suit, and slid his hand into Pierce's inner pocket.

"Excuse me!" Pierce exclaimed and moved his hand to stop the assault, but Mayer slapped it away, then he extracted the silver cigarette case and held it up in front of Pierce.

"What about this?"

"I don't know what you're . . ."

"Can the act," Mayer said, interrupting. "We don't have time for tall tales and fables."

Pierce's face sank. "All right, I took it from him," he admitted. "I've always admired it and it didn't mean anything to him. He told me it was a gift from an old girlfriend."

"So you slipped it out of the dead man's suit coat?"

"Sure," Pierce said, screwing up his courage. "Why not? He wasn't going to need it anymore."

Mayer slipped the case into his own suit coat. "C'mon," he said. "We'd better head out."

"Do you have to destroy it?" Pierce asked. "I would certainly not like to see that happen."

"We'll see," Mayer said.

The drive to the shaman's house was made mostly in silence as Mayer pondered about what type of man was sitting next to him. Someone who would steal from a dead man—a once partner—without any sign of remorse. If Pierce was willing to do that, Mayer wondered what else he might be willing to do. He also wondered why the cigarette case seemed so important to him, and why he downplayed its importance to his partner.

They arrived at the shaman's home, parked out front, and went to the door. Mayer noted that Cassi's Fairlane was absent. It was a safe bet she would be as well.

"Where are we?" Pierce asked.

"A safe place," Mayer said and knocked on the door. He was surprised when the shaman answered to see him none the worse for wear. Not that he knew what to expect, but he was surprisingly spry for a man who just had a near-death experience. He shook the shaman's hand and made the necessary introductions. The shaman offered to take Pierce's hat and suit coat. Pierce handed him the hat, then made a bit of a face as he pulled off the coat.

"Injured?" asked the shaman.

"He took a pill to the shoulder," Mayer said. "But it just grazed him."

"Perhaps I should take a look. Do you mind removing your shirt, Mr. Pierce?"

Pierce looked to Mayer with concern.

"Go on," Mayer said. "He's a shaman. A Native American healer. He won't bite."

Pierce nodded then removed his tie and shirt, laying them both on the back of the nearest chair.

The shaman had a look at the injury. "Yes," he said. "I can definitely help with that."

"If he offers you tea, don't take it," Mayer cautioned and took a seat in one of the empty chairs.

Diogie raised his head, growled, then lowered it again.

"I don't think your dog likes me," Mayer said.

"It's not you he doesn't like. It's the dark energy that surrounds you."

"Dandy."

The shaman mixed several herbs into a paste, then attended to Pierce's wound.

"You didn't tell me the skinwalker could transform into people from someone else's past," Mayer said.

"That's because they can't," the shaman answered casually. "They can mimic voices, but I've never heard of them transforming like that."

"Well, it had the voice of my mother and it was a female."

The shaman stopped what he was doing and focused on Mayer. "What do you mean it was a female?"

"I tried your trick, you know, getting it to talk while in animal form. I goaded it on, trying to make it mad, hoping it would say something and be forced to transform back into a human."

"What happened?" the shaman asked.

"I'm afraid *I* did," Pierce said.

"That's right," Mayer confirmed. "He yelled at me to shoot the thing and gummed up the plan. It got distracted and that was that."

"That's a shame," the shaman said.

"I tried to shoot, Mayer continued, "but like before, my gun jammed. And right after that happened, I heard my dead mother's voice and the thing transformed into a woman—or maybe that happened first, I'm not sure. It might have been my mother, or it might not have been. It was hard to tell, because it was covered in painted symbols, but it was definitely female."

"Are you sure?" the shaman asked, forcefully.

"Look, I may not know a lot of things, but I think I know a female when I see one."

"And you say it spoke to you in your mother's voice?"

"Yes, had me transfixed too. I almost shot myself in the head with my own piece. I knew I was doing it too, but I couldn't stop myself."

"How *did* you stop?"

"Well, I'm not entirely sure, but I think it saw my tattoo and got scared."

"Tattoo?"

Mayer stood and pulled up his sleeve, revealing the Helm of Awe tattoo on his forearm.

"Are you of Viking descent?" the shaman asked as he examined Mayer's arm.

"Not a bit," Mayer said. "I found the symbol in my mother's diary. I did some additional research and discovered that it protects against injustice and evil. Thought it might come in handy some day."

"And so it has," the shaman said. "The symbol protects the bearer by striking fear into his enemy. It is associated with the power of the serpent who paralyzes its prey before striking."

"That explains it," Mayer said.

"What does it explain?" the shaman asked.

"The creature froze when it saw the thing. After a few moments, it let out a hellish scream, then transformed back into its coyote form before it blew.

The shaman nodded. "Probably screamed to break the hold the symbol had on it," he said, then added, "You got lucky this time. I thought I told you not to go at it alone."

"It's not like I had a choice," Mayer said. "It came to me, not the other way around. Mayer glanced at Pierce. He sat, looking distant, a strange expression on his face. "That reminds me," Mayer said and pulled the cigarette case out of his pocket. "You got any way of separating a ghost from an object?"

"Destroy it," the shaman said and returned his attention to Pierce.

"No soap," Mayer said. "Pierce wants to keep the item."

The shaman tore a scrap of cloth and placed it over the paste, then told Pierce he could get dressed, but suggested he might be more comfortable without the tie. Mayer handed him the cigarette case. The shaman examined the outside, then opened it and did the same with the interior portion.

"Why is this so special?" he asked Pierce.

"It's not that it's special, per se," Pierce said. "I've just grown partial to it is all."

The shaman gave Pierce suspicious eyes. Mayer couldn't blame him.

"There is a ceremony," the shaman admitted, "but I cannot guarantee its effectiveness. It would probably be best to just destroy it."

"I'd prefer that you didn't," Pierce said.

"Try it," Mayer said. "I'll take the case with me. If Hawthorne comes back for it, I'll know what to do."

"Very well," The shaman said. He took the case over to his table of herbs, lit the sage, and let the smoke encompass the case. He said several words that neither Pierce nor Mayer understood, then placed the case between his hands, brought them to his mouth, and blew. When he was done, he handed the case back to Mayer.

"I'll keep it warm for you," Mayer said to Pierce.

"What are your plans now?" the shaman asked. "Please don't tell me you are going after the witch."

"Not tonight," Mayer admitted. "I need some shuteye and time to think."

"You're welcome to stay here," the shaman offered.

"I appreciate the offer. But I'm partial to my own bed," Mayer said and walked to the door.

Diogie growled.

"As you wish," the shaman said.

"How long must I stay here?" Pierce asked.

"Just until I kill the thing," Mayer said. He took hold of the doorknob and asked the shaman, "Will you be safe here?" Mayer asked. "We don't want another corpse powder incident."

"We will be safe," the shaman assured him. "The elders have helped me place protection spells on the house and property. If the witch comes, it will not make it to the front door."

"You up for this?"

"When the time comes, I will be ready."

Mayer nodded. He opened the door and stepped outside. The shaman followed. He was about to get into his car when a thought occurred to him. "Didn't you tell me the skinwalker can't come inside a house unless invited?"

"Yes, that is true," the shaman confirmed.

"Then how did one jump through the window of William James Pierce's home?" Mayer didn't wait for an answer. He climbed behind the wheel and headed to Las Vegas. He had a stop to make before the night was through.

23

MAYER DROVE STRAIGHT back to Pierce's house, parked in the circular drive, and got out. Then he reloaded the Colt with the silver bullets he kept under the front seat—just in case. He took off his suit coat and lid, placed them on the front seat, and rolled up his sleeves, making sure the tattoo was exposed. If the skinwalker came back, he wanted to be ready, though, to be honest, he was far more worried about Hawthorne's ghost. He wasn't sure the tattoo would have the same effect on the ghost that it had had on the skinwalker—what, after all did the dead have to fear—but he did it all the same.

He also took out the iron club he kept in the trunk, reasoning it would be more effective than the poker. After he had all the tools he needed, Mayer closed and locked the trunk. He had no sooner done so when he felt the first drops.

The moon fought the clouds for dominance. Rain in Las Vegas was a curious thing. Unlike most places, clouds weren't necessary for rain to fall. In fact, Las Vegas was likely the only place in the world where a nice, sunny, blue-sky, white-cloud day could produce rain. But the sky wasn't blue and the clouds weren't white and when it rained in Las Vegas it followed the old adage and poured. He hoped it wasn't a sign of things to come.

A strong wind—as winds tend to do—blew in from the north, as a bolt of lightning lit the night sky. In another second the lights died, leaving the entire block in darkness. Mayer opened the trunk, removed a flashlight, and closed it again. Then he braced himself against the wind and headed inside. Rich people are so accustomed to someone else taking care of such things as locking front doors, that Pierce didn't even notice Mayer had left it unsecured. It was a good thing Mayer was on the man's side, or he could have rolled the place.

With its only occupant absent, the quiet in the home was a sharp contrast to the storm brewing outside. The air inside was still. Jagged pieces of a vase lay where they landed after a bullet sliced through. Plywood protected a glassless window. Mayer sidestepped the dark stain on the wood floor near the entrance. He tried the light switch, just in case, without result. Most people would have turned on their torch to vanquish the dark, but not Mayer. He liked the dark. It comforted him. He didn't want the party crashed, so he locked the door behind him.

When he came the first time, Mayer had only a cursory look at the place. Now he had time to take a better look. Except for the recent muck, Pierce's house was surprisingly clean for a bachelor. A place for everything and everything in its place. The benefits of daily maid service—something Mayer would likely never be privileged enough to enjoy. But it was all right, he liked his place just the way it was—lived in.

And that, Mayer suddenly realized, was what was missing. While the walls were replete with bibelots, gewgaws, and trinkets, it had no warmth. Vacant were family photographs of any type. No mother. No father. No nieces, nephews, or even friends. Nothing to denote that the place was even inhabited. As antiseptic as a department store showroom. And, as clean as it was, there existed a lingering, rather unpleasant odor, one Mayer couldn't quite put his finger on.

With the club on his shoulder, Mayer made his way to the spiral staircase leading to the second floor. Seeing none on the first floor, the bedrooms, Mayer assumed, were upstairs. He hoped an office would be there as well. He wouldn't be disappointed.

When a house is empty, things like a metal staircase—especially a spiral one—make more than their fair share of noise. Every footstep Mayer took echoed as if the leg taking the step was burdened with excessive weight. A sledgehammer striking each metal tread. Despite himself, Mayer stepped even lighter than usual until he reached the top.

The office was at the end of a long hallway, next to what he assumed was the master bedroom. A flick of the switch brought the flashlight to life. The office wasn't as clean as the rest of the house, which likely meant the housekeeper wasn't allowed inside. That didn't surprise Mayer. Pierce seemed like the kind of guy who didn't take to prying eyes.

The office was equipped with the usual trappings. A lavish desk faced the door, a heavy wooden chair resting between it and file cabinets which occupied the entire wall behind the desk. Atop the desk was a phone, a wheeldex, and a fancy pen set that was missing one of the pens. The wall to the right was decorated with various photos of Pierce posing with what were likely important people. Finally something to show the house had life.

Rain battered the window. Lightning lit the room. Mayer settled into the heavy wooden chair behind the desk, resting the club within reach, and began opening drawers. He wasn't sure just what he was looking for, but he knew there was something that needed to be found. Something that would help this all make sense. He was beginning to suspect there was more to this whole thing than a skinwalker protecting sacred land. In fact, the more he thought about it, the more he was convinced that sacred land had nothing at all to do with it. Why would a witch bent on mischief, greed, and destruction care one bit for something sacred? It just didn't sit well with him.

There was nothing in any of the drawers that caught Mayer's eye. Nothing that explained what Hawthorne's ghost meant when he said: "I know what you did, William, and I know why you did it." Even though it was the skinwalker who actually said it, not Hawthorne, it had a ring of truth.

Not being able to find anything worthwhile, Mayer turned his attention to the cigarette case, taking it from his pocket and setting it atop the desk. The ornate case was decorated with flowing leaves that swirled in delicate circles across the face. The rear portion was slightly curved to conform to the body when placed in the inner pocket of a suit. It had a hinge along one edge and a clasp on the other.

Mayer pressed the clasp and opened the case. Inside he found a row of slim, brown cigarettes standing at the ready in the curved side. They were held in place by an elastic band positioned toward the top. He took them out one by one and laid them on Pierce's desk. With the cigarettes removed, Mayer could see both the maker's mark, as well as an inscription that read: "To R. J. with all my love, your geliebte."

"Why," Mayer wondered aloud, "would someone put the engraving on the cigarette side of the case where it wouldn't be seen?" But that wasn't the only thing he wondered. The word "geliebte" caught his attention as well. He didn't know the meaning of the word, but he was pretty sure he knew the origin.

He turned next to the file cabinets, searching each drawer, unsure of what he was supposed to find. Still, he kept looking, hoping that whatever it was would announce itself with a fine how d'ya do. But it never did.

Thunder cracked as lightening brightened the sky. As a kid, Mayer had been frightened of thunder—especially at night. His mother would come into his room to comfort him, telling him the noise was only the angels bowling and was nothing to be frightened of. Louder bangs were simply strikes. One particular strike hit hard, coming almost immediately after the lightning that preceded it, bringing with it a tinge of that old fear.

He swiveled the chair back to the desk. Large enough to serve as a dining table for a family of six, the ornate wooden desk was equipped with six drawers. A set of three on each side had pull handles, with an additional, smaller knob-handled drawer above each set of three. The drawer in the top center was secured with a lock.

It likely took four hardy men and a team of Clydesdales to get the thing into the place, which made Mayer wonder how they managed to carry it up the spiral staircase. The one-of-a-kind desk was the type a man chose to flaunt his wealth. He was also pretty sure it was the type that came with a secret compartment or two. Though he'd already given it the once over, Mayer took his time on the second go round. He started with the drawers on the right side, figuring most people were right handed. He would have started with the center drawer at the top, but that seemed too obvious. Wise people don't keep important things in a locked drawer, it's the first place a man like Mayer would check.

He pulled open the top right drawer. It was filled with miscellaneous junk: an old pipe, matches, lighter fluid, pencils, an engraved letter opener, the missing pen from the set, and close to two berries in change. He slipped the drawer out of its spot, looked underneath and at the end. A single groove ran around the outside of the drawer, but other than that, nothing caught his eye. He returned the drawer and its contents. The next two were much of the same. The third drawer was mostly empty, except for a box of Cubans. He lifted the lid. A single row remained. He was about to slide the drawer back into place when he noticed something odd. Though the face of the drawer was the same size as the two above it, the drawer itself wasn't as deep. There wasn't a big difference; not one that'd be noticed if a person wasn't paying attention. But if that person were paying attention, if someone really looked closely, the difference was just enough to catch the eye.

Mayer removed the box of Cubans and laid them on the top of the desk, then he took out the drawer. He examined the inside, but found nothing out of the ordinary, so he turned the thing over. The bottom of the drawer had a slight indentation at one end—something that could be used to slide the bottom piece forward or backward as needed. Only it didn't slide much—maybe a fraction of an inch—before it hit either the back or front of the drawer. It could have been that the bottom piece was simply old and becoming loose, but it didn't feel that way.

Mayer tried wiggling the bottom, but it didn't help. He examined the outside of the drawer and found two grooves that ran along the sides and the end. *Two grooves,* Mayer thought. *Each of the other drawers had only one groove.*

Lightening lit the room.

He took hold of the end of the drawer and pulled upward. Much to his delight, a small piece came loose, allowing Mayer to slide out the bottom of the drawer as well, exposing a large manila envelope. He placed the envelope on the desk, opened the top flap, and poured out its contents.

Photos. It was full of photos. Two people—a man and a woman—sometimes walking hand in hand, other times on horseback. Once or twice locking lips. Most of them were taken from a distance, but it was still possible to identify the subjects. A fairly well-known woman, one Mayer had spoken with only the day before. Vera Krupp.

The man wasn't as easy to identify, but his clothes were. A long-sleeve button-down shirt with flaps over the pockets, twist twill slacks, a covert-cloth jacket, and engineer boots. They were the same clothes Mayer had seen in a suitcase in the trailer when Pierce first took him there.

"Well how d'ya do?" Mayer said.

Inside the envelope, along with the photos, was a folded slip of paper. A receipt for services rendered—two hundred dollars. Pierce had hired a private peeper to tail his partner. Mayer wondered if his client had trust issues. He slid the receipt back into the envelope along with the photos. Then he put the drawer together and slid in back in the desk. He was about to head for the door when the hairs stood up on his arms, a cold chill swept down his spine, and his breath trailed off in front of him.

He took hold of the club.

Lightening flashed and as it did, Mayer saw it. Standing in the entry to the office, floating just inches above the floor, was the same specter he'd seen earlier that evening in the living room—Hawthorne's ghost. Malice and revenge painted his face. Clearly the shaman's trick hadn't worked.

"I'm afraid you've got the wrong bird," Mayer said.

The ghost didn't answer. It simply flickered as it did before, and when it did, the light in his torch went dark, and with it, the room. Mayer looked to the window, hoping a skinwalker wasn't about to come crashing through. But as he did, the window disappeared. In fact, everything in the room dissolved away, replaced with a thick darkness so heavy it became difficult to breathe.

Mayer put down the torch and held up his hand in front of his face, but even though it was a mere inches away, it was impossible to see.

He stood silently, trying to let his ears do the work of his eyes, tuning in even the slightest sound. A cold breeze scraped across the back of his neck, raising the hairs. Though he couldn't see him, Mayer could feel Hawthorne quickly closing the distance between them. His grip tightened on the club. Then a sound—metal sliding along metal—came from behind him, accompanied by more of the same. A second later Mayer was bombarded by papers and folders, all falling from the sky.

He went to move, but one of the desk drawers flung forward, catching him in the shin. The unexpected movement and the sharp pain it brought dropped Mayer to the floor, just as another drawer struck him in the chest and a third in the forehead. The club slipped from his grasp, lost in the darkness.

On the floor and disoriented, Mayer tried to catch his breath. It was there, lying on the papers and folders, that he heard the creak of the heavy wooden chair, and suddenly realized it had been lifted off the floor. Mayer had a fairly good idea what the ghost intended to do with the chair but didn't wait to find out. He reached until he found the corner of the desk, then, keeping his hand in place to orient himself, Mayer rolled around the desk and came up on the other side. The room echoed when the chair slammed to the floor.

Mayer tried to take in air but his chest was tight. His shin was aching and he was pretty sure blood was dripping from his forehead. He concentrated on his ears, painting a picture with sound. A brush of wind, a stir of dust. The slightest movement in the air. But all he could hear was the pounding beat of his own heart.

Keeping his hands on the desk, Mayer turned slightly, facing what he thought was the position of the door. From out of the darkness, something hit him hard in the chest, sending him flying across the desk. He landed hard on the floor; two objects fell on top of him.

He fumbled for them. One felt like the cigarette case and the other a large envelope. He slipped the case into his back pocket and took hold of the envelope. Though he felt sick to his stomach, Mayer knew he couldn't wait for the ghost to strike again. He managed to get to his knees, then peeked over Pierce's desk, but it was still too dark for him to see.

Lightning struck. A slight flash fought against the darkness that filled the room and forced itself in, just enough for Mayer to catch a glimpse of the club. It had rolled to the wall just under the window. But the lightning also revealed Hawthorne hovering above him. The ghost raised his hand and pointed a missing forefinger at Mayer. Then a swipe of the hand sent Mayer flying; he hit the wall with a dull thud. But now Mayer had the club. He took hold of it and rushed where Hawthorne had been, swinging it out in front of him. But the darkness had once again engulfed the room, leaving Mayer to wonder if his swing had made any difference.

Mayer turned to where he thought the door should be, but as he did, he heard it slam shut.

"Damn ghosts," he said.

He realized that even if he could get to the door and get it to open, he'd still be in the house and he'd still have to deal with Hawthorne's ghost. But there was another way out.

He moved, arms outstretched, until he felt the wall. Then he followed along, by envelope-clad hand, until he could feel the cold glass of the window. A scraping of metal echoed in the room, bringing with it a sense of urgency. Mayer lifted the club and slammed it into the windowpane. While glass rained down, he leapt out, just as a file cabinet came flying toward him. He tucked his legs tight to his chest, as the cabinet inched by, and rolled out onto the roof.

Once out of the window, the glass, rain, and wet asphalt shingles conspired against him, making it impossible for Mayer to get to his feet or stop his forward momentum, so he braced for impact as he slipped off the edge of the roof, faceplanting into the ground—lucky to have landed on the grass and not the cement walkway only inches away.

Gasping for air, Mayer got to his hands and knees, then, eventually, his feet. Somehow he had managed to keep hold of the envelope, but had lost the club. Though it was night, outside the home was much lighter than inside—even with the power out. Seeing the club a few feet away, he grabbed it, ran to his Hornet, opened the door, and threw himself inside. Without taking a breath, he slid the key into the ignition, started the engine, slammed the gas pedal, and skidded away.

24

MAYER PULLED IN front of his apartment and turned off the ignition. He sat there in the dark, finally allowing himself to breathe. The rain had stopped and the streets glistened with the reflection of neon signs and streetlights that kept the twenty-four-hour town illuminated.

Atomic Liquors was one of those lights—its doors still open, people still inside, lying to each other, with glasses full, going over the edge with the rams. Almost as if nothing had happened. Almost as if Mayer hadn't just been attacked by a dead man's ghost or a Native American hellcat. Almost as if Vegas was like any other town in America and not a gathering place for the unnatural. And while Mayer was in no mood to join them, he needed to use the phone. So, after depositing his club and Colt in the trunk and donning his suit coat and lid, Mayer headed inside.

The place was busy and Mayer was thankful for it— less time to get a lecture from Stella. He took a quick scan of the room. Stella was in the far corner talking to a table full of Air Force men in pressed suits, one of them sporting a sleeve full of stripes, their flight caps tucked inside their belts. Joe was behind the bar. He caught Mayer's eye and waved him in.

"Geez, you look worse than the last time I saw you," he said when Mayer reached the bar. "I didn't think that was possible."

"Anything's possible," Mayer said. "If you try hard enough."

Joe wiped the bar in front of Mayer out of habit. He motioned to his grass-stained shirt, still wet from the rain-soaked lawn. "What'd you do, nap in a park?"

"Something like that."

"Go freshen up and I'll pour you a drink," Joe said, jerking a nod at the restroom in the back. Mayer was halfway there when Joe added, "That reporter is looking for you. The cute one with the pixie-cut hair."

"Dandy," Mayer said.

When he got to the restroom, he went to the sink, trying his best to avoid the mirror. He turned on the water and let it get hot, before lathering his face with soap and splashing it with water. He did it several more times hoping to wash off both the dirt and the evening in general. It worked for the dirt, but not the other. He'd probably have to tip a few for that.

When Mayer got back to the bar, a short glass of rum was waiting for him. Joe knew just what he needed. A piece of paper with a phone number was wedged under the drink. Mayer took a snort and then took another. Rum had a way of making things no longer matter— perfect for a night like tonight.

Mayer's first call was to the shaman. He wanted to let Pierce know he had another window broken, but declined to speak with him when the shaman offered, not wanting to explain how he came about that particular piece of information. He left out the ghost and pretty much everything else except the broken window.

His next call was to Cassie.

"We need to talk," she said after pleasantries.

"Not tonight," Mayer said.

"First thing in the morning then. I've got news you're going to want to hear."

"You remember where Atomic Liquors is?"

"Don't be cute."

"My apartment's right behind the place. Come in the morning, but not too early." Mayer hung up before Cassi could answer. Stella was still occupied with guests and Mayer didn't want to be there when she got free. It wasn't that he was hiding from her. He just didn't want to go into the whole mess right then; at least that's what he told himself. His bed was calling like the sirens to Odysseus, only Mayer fully intended to answer the call.

He slammed down the rest of his drink, exited stage left, and went to his apartment, stopping only briefly at the Hornet to get the envelope he'd found in Pierce's office. Once inside, he placed the envelope on the small table in the kitchenette, along with his lid. Then he pulled the cigarette case from his pants pocket and tossed it onto the bed.

In the kitchen he took a tin of salt and spread it across the panes of all his windows and refreshed it along the threshold of the only door leading out. Not having invited the thing in, he wasn't as worried about the skinwalker as he was about Hawthorne. Ghosts didn't need invitations. They also weren't stopped by salt at doors and windows.

Mayer was beginning to suspect that Hawthorne wasn't as tied to the cigarette case as he initially suspected. After all, the ghost didn't appear in the car on the way to his apartment. It also hadn't made an appearance at the shaman's house while the case was there. Added to that was Pierce's clear fear at seeing the ghost of his partner for the first time, yet he'd had the case in his pocket for days since the man's demise. So while he was pretty sure the ghost wouldn't make an appearance, Mayer surrounded the bed with a ring of salt just for good measure. He also kept another iron club by the head of the bed and a .45 under the pillow, just in case unexpected visitors came to call.

He removed his suit coat, holster, and shirt and placed them over the back of the chair. Then he kicked off his shoes, dropped his trousers, stepped over the ring of salt, and fell into bed. Sleep came fast that night, but it wasn't one that gave Mayer any peace. The rum in his gut twisted his dreams into a hole too black to crawl out of and too bleak to stay in, as he wrestled with visions of a past that would never set him free.

25

"COME NOW PROMETHEUS, what are those tears for?" his mother asked, wiping his eyes with a gentle hand.

"But I don't want you to go," Mayer said, looking down at his socked feet hanging from the side of the bed. One was black and the other blue.

His mother smiled. She had the kindest smile—the type of smile that lit the entire face and made the eyes sparkle. The type that could make a young boy happy, no matter what the world cast at him. When the kids at school started calling him "Night Mayer," it was his mother who calmed him down with her smile.

"Prometheus is a proud name," she told him. "One of the Titans. The god of fire. Your name means forethought, and it was your namesake who gave man the gifts they needed to survive once they were formed from clay. It was Prometheus who fought alongside Zeus in the battle for the heavens."

Of course it would be much later in life when Mayer would discover that it was, in fact, that same Prometheus—known as the clever trickster—who started that very battle and fought with the Titans against Zeus, eventually defecting to the other side when he grew irritated with the Titans' refusal to use his tactics. But none of that mattered. When Mayer was with his mother, nothing in the world could hurt him.

"Why can't I go with you?"

She lifted her son's chin. "Now Prometheus, you know you can't come with us. Your father and I have work to do. Besides, who would Helen and Stella have to play with if you left?"

"Will you come back?"

She rose, went to the window, and pulled the curtains aside. After a moment, she turned to him and smiled. "No, Prometheus," she said. "Not this time."

That's when Mayer heard it. The pounding of heeled boots in step. A menacing death march goose-stepping toward them, ever closer. Louder and louder. The sound of a thousand soldiers marching in step. Stomp, stomp, STOMP.

SEVERAL MINUTES PASSED before Mayer realized the sound was coming from his front door. A knocking, well before he was awake, and long before he'd had his coffee.

"Go away," Mayer shouted, but the knocking continued.

"Open up, Mayer," the female voice called from the other side. "I know you're in there."

"Mayer's dead. Let him rest in peace."

The knocking continued, so much so that Mayer had little choice but to rise and let his disrupter enter. He slipped on his trousers and stumbled shirtless to the door, his hair a rat's nest atop his head. Waiting for him on the other side was Cassi in a red and white sleeveless blouse and gaucho pants. Cheaters covered her eyes and she held a gasper loosely between her red lips. Along with her purse, she carried—to her enduring benefit—a steaming cup of Joe.

"You look like hell," she commented and handed him the cup. "Stella said you'd need this."

Mayer took the offering and moved aside to let Cassi in, warning her to step over the salt barrier. She did, exaggerating the move, as if afraid to get something unpleasant on her shoes. Once inside, she gave the place the once over.

"Quaint," she said. "Use enough salt?"

"Protection against unwanted visitors," Mayer explained. "Doesn't always work."

"Hey, *you* invited *me*."

He sipped the coffee, then donned his grass-stained shirt just for a cover, leaving the shoulder holster draped over the chair. "Have you eaten?" he asked.

"No."

"Give me a chance to look presentable and I'll take you to breakfast. Make yourself at home."

Cassi crinkled her nose. "Unlikely," she said.

Mayer showered, but decided to skip the shave. He combed his hair, tucked a fresh shirt into his trousers, picked out a tie, and tightened his belt. When he emerged from the small bathroom, he found Cassi straightening up the place. "What are you doing?" he asked.

"Playing the housekeeper," she said. "You could use one of those."

"I could use a two-week vacation in Tahiti," Mayer said, as he got into his shoulder holster, "but it isn't likely." He removed the cigarette case from the bed and placed it in the inside pocket of his suit coat, put on the coat, and placed his hat in position atop his newly-combed hair.

"You coming?" he asked, as he picked up the envelope and headed for the door.

Cassi followed him out and over to his Hornet. He held the door open for her, just like his father had taught him, then went to the driver's seat. He pulled out of the parking lot, turned left on Fremont and headed to a little diner he favored. The pair entered and took a booth. A middle-aged waitress in a pink uniform with a white, food-stained apron tied around her ample middle tossed menus on the table. "Coffee?" she asked.

Mayer nodded.

Before they could even get a good look at the menu, she'd returned, sliding the coffee in front of them. "What'll you have?" she asked.

Mayer put down the menu. "I'll have two poached on toast," he said. "And a donut for my coffee."

"Adam and Eve on a raft and a life preserver!" the waitress called out, writing on a notepad. "And you dear?"

"How about French toast," Cassi said.

"You want eggs?"

"Sure, scrambled please."

"Biddy board with machine oil and two cackleberries! Wreck 'em!" the waitress called as she walked away.

"You come here often?" Cassi asked after the waitress left.

"Often enough," Mayer said, sipping his coffee. "What have you got for me?"

Cassi pulled the notepad from her purse and began turning pages. "Well, this took a bit of work, but I think I found a connection to a Navajo in the area."

"Did you now?"

"I found a story from the late 1800's about a woman who was wanted for the brutal murder of her children and husband—killed them with a hunting knife in the middle of the night! Her name was Hak'az Asdzą́ą́," Cassi said, likely butchering the name. "She was ostracized by the tribe and labeled a witch. The Navajo County Sheriff's Department in Arizona searched for her for days. They tracked her across the state, but lost her somewhere in

Mohave County, near Kingman. They think she crossed into Nevada, but could never prove it. They found a campsite they believed to be hers, but all that was left were the carcasses of several skinned animals."

"Let me guess, coyotes?"

Cassi tapped her nose.

"But that would mean our skinwalker is a wom . . ." He stopped without finishing his sentence and it was then that Mayer realized the witch hadn't transformed into his mother at all. She had simply changed back into her own female body. The only part that was his mother was the voice.

"You okay?" Cassi asked.

"I had another run-in with the skinwalker last night. It transformed into my mother. At least I thought it was my mother."

"I didn't think it could do that."

"It can't, according to the shaman. But it was a woman. When it transformed from beast to human, it was in the form of a woman."

"Why did you think it was your mother?"

"It spoke in her voice. When it transformed, I just assumed it was her. But it wasn't, was it? Our skinwalker is a woman."

"That's what I've been trying to tell you, Mayer. It's a woman and her name is Hak'az Asdzą́ą́."

"Great, but how did she get to Las Vegas?"

"Be patient," Cassi said. "Several years later there was a story about a Paiute shaman by the name of Wovoka who worked tirelessly to protect the sacred Paiute area just below the Red Rock Escarpment. He had a wife who died of cholera and a daughter named Thocmentony—Tony for short."

"I don't see the connection," Mayer admitted.

"Neither did I," Cassi continued. "Until I found other records that revealed more about the shaman and his family. His first wife died shortly after the birth of their daughter. He later married a Navajo woman. It was quite a controversy in the tribe—a Paiute healer marrying a Navajo. She too was a healer. Her name was listed as Giiwedinokwe, but according to the records, she took the Paiute name Besa-Yoona when she married.

"So?" Mayer asked.

"Giiwedinokwe is not a Navajo name. It's Ojibwe."

"Okay, so her parents liked the name. There's no harm in that."

"Except Giiwedinokwe translates to "woman of the north," and Hak'az Asdzą́ą́ means "cold woman.""

"That's too close of a coincidence," Mayer said.

"That's what I think."

"So Hak'az Asdzą́ą́ has been living here all along under the name Besa-Yoona?"

"It would appear so," Cassi said.

"You tell any of this to the shaman?"

Cassi shook her head. "I never really got the chance. After he felt better, I let him rest. Besides, I wanted to tell you first."

"Well, that's one mystery solved." Mayer said.

"What's the other?"

"Why she's killing people who come on that land."

The waitress returned with their food and laid it down on the table.

"Simple," Cassi said after she left. "She's carrying on the work of her husband and protecting sacred land."

"I don't buy it. That would be a selfless act. It doesn't sound like the creature the shaman described. A person with no redeeming value, possessed by greed, anger, envy, and spite—often revenge. A person that had its heart and soul overtaken with blackness. Someone who must continually kill or perish itself."

"Well, if it's not protecting the land, why are all the deaths in the area associated with construction on sacred land?"

It was a good question, but Mayer had no answer. "Maybe this is a clue," he said, then opened the envelope and poured its contents out on the table.

"What's this?" Cassi asked.

"Photographs of Vera Krupp and R. J. Hawthorne. The mystery man your friend in the sheriff's department told you about. I found them in Pierce's office." He handed Cassi the receipt. "Paid two hundred big ones for a peeper to tail his partner around. And then there's this." he said and pulled the cigarette case out from his inside coat pocket, then handed it to Cassi. "Go ahead. Open it."

Cassi did as Mayer said and found the engraving. She read it aloud. "To R. J. with all my love, your geliebte."

"Don't know what geliebte means, but I'd take odds it's German."

"So Hawthorne was having an affair with Vera Krupp?"

"Looks that way."

"Yet she was trying to thwart his plans for development." She turned a few pages in her notepad. "Mostly unsuccessfully. The courts repeatedly ruled against her, that is, until she managed to enlist an environmental group who told her the area was the habitat of the desert orangetip."

"Desert orangetip?" Mayer questioned.

"A butterfly native to the region. With the help of the group, she managed to get an injunction. Put the project on hold."

"I bet that frosted Pierce but good."

"Probably, but it was unlikely to have any lasting effect. The court only gave two months for the study. She caught a break with that suicide note."

"Didn't she though," Mayer said.

Cassi took to her French toast. "You said you had another run-in with the skinwalker," she said between bites. "I hope you didn't go back to that cave alone."

Mayer shook his head. "I was at Pierce's house with him and his hired man when the skinwalker came crashing through the window, but before it did, Hawthorne's ghost appeared and attacked Pierce. Hawthorne's voice said, 'I know what you did and why you did it.'"

"His voice?"

"Yeah, it was Hawthorne's voice, according to Pierce, but it didn't come from the ghost. It's been my experience that some ghosts speak and some don't. Mostly the ones with malicious intent don't. I guess it's more fun that way."

"If the voice wasn't coming from Hawthorne's ghost, then it must have been . . ."

"The skinwalker," Mayer said, finishing her sentence.

"What do you think it was referring to?"

Mayer picked up his life preserver and dunked it into his cup of Joe, then took a bite. "I'm not sure yet," he said with a mouth full of donut, "but there are a couple of things that bug me. Like why was the skinwalker able to come crashing through the window? The shaman said it couldn't enter a house unless it was invited . . ." Mayer paused, the words hitting him for the first time: *a skinwalker couldn't enter a house unless invited. A house . . . or a trailer.* It was something he had missed. The skinwalker could not have come into the trailer uninvited. So, Mayer wondered, *who invited it in?*

"You still with me?" Cassi asked.

The question brought Mayer back. "Where was I?"

"Something about the skinwalker needing to be invited."

"Right," Mayer said. "But it scared the devil out of Pierce, so unless he's some great actor, I'd say he'd never seen the thing before." Mayer took hold of the cigarette case with his free hand. "And why was Pierce so terribly fond of this cigarette case? So fond that he didn't want it destroyed?"

"Why would it be destroyed?"

Mayer told Cassi about the case. How Pierce had removed it from his partner's dead body and how he was adamant that it remain intact, how the shaman performed a ritual to cleanse the case and break the chain between it and Hawthorne's ghost.

"Did it work?"

"I'm not even sure it was necessary in the first place." Mayer said and took another bite of donut. "But skinwalkers can read minds, that's how it knew my mother's voice and that's how it knew what it was that Pierce had done to Hawthorne."

"So what do we do now?"

Mayer smiled. "We find out exactly what it was the skinwalker discovered about Pierce."

26

UPON FINISHING BREAKFAST, Mayer drove Cassi out to Diamond V Ranch. The trip was mostly quiet with Mayer running everything through his head and, he suspected, Cassi doing the same from her angle. Mayer had many questions for Mrs. Krupp, not the least of which involved the amulet he found in his mother's diary. That, however, was a subject he wasn't quite sure how to broach.

As they turned onto the dirt road leading to the ranch, Mayer decided not to tell Cassi about the amulet or its apparent connection to Krupp's husband and his penchant for the occult—that was best left between him and Vera. When they reached the ranch house, Mayer parked in the drive, put his lid in place, and removed the envelope from the seat. Then he walked Cassi up the path toward the house. They had made it most of the way before running into Buster, who was on his knees collecting dandelions and placing them in a metal bucket.

He looked up at Mayer through dark cheaters. "Ah, Mr. Mayer. You have come back."

Mayer found it interesting that Krupp's hired man knew his name. He didn't remember introducing himself on his first visit until after the man left. "That I have," he said.

Buster stood, removed his gloves, then used them to brush off the knees of his dungarees. "Have you come for Mrs. Krupp or for the witch?"

"Excuse me?" Mayer said, more than a little taken aback.

"That's quite enough," a female voice said. It was a voice Mayer had heard before, one that belonged to Vera's gatekeeper, Peg Westburg. "You may go now, Buster."

Buster nodded. He picked up his bucket of dandelions and turned to leave, but before he did, he lowered his cheaters and winked at Mayer.

"What was that about?" Mayer asked Vera Krupp's secretary.

"Nothing of significance," she said, giving the pair the once over. "Is there something I can help you with, Mr. Mayer?"

"I, that is we, Miss Reyes and I, came to see Mrs. Krupp."

"Have you an appointment?" she asked through tight lips, clutching a stack of folders to her chest.

"We do not," Mayer admitted, then added, "But she said I could come back."

"That was two days ago."

"I'm no good with time."

Krupp's secretary gave Mayer stern eyes. He didn't mind.

"We only have a few questions," Cassi offered.

Peg Westburg turned sharply. "Cassi Reyes," she said, more as an accusation than a statement. "Reporter for the *Las Vegas Morning Sun*?"

"Yes," Cassi admitted more sheepishly than needed.

"Are you here on official business?"

"She's not here to write an article if that's what you're getting at," Mayer offered. "She's helping me with my case."

"Ah, yes. The one for which Mr. Pierce hired you."

Peg Westburg was proving her worth as a gatekeeper, but Mayer was running out of patience and he was about to let her know it, when she said, "Wait here and I will see if Mrs. Krupp is willing to entertain you. If not, you will be expected to leave."

She didn't wait for a response, but marched up to the house and disappeared inside. Mayer and Cassi waited.

"What do you think Buster meant?" Cassi asked.

Mayer jerked a thumb toward the door Peg Westburg had just entered. "I think he meant her."

"Really, Mayer!"

Cassi likely would have said more if Vera's gatekeeper hadn't appeared at the door and waved them in. "Mrs. Krupp will see you."

Mayer guided Cassi through the door with a hand and tipped his hat to Peg Westburg as he entered. Vera Krupp was waiting for them in the front room. It was quite a sight. Timbers supported an exposed ceiling atop sandstone walls. A large, well-used, brick fireplace with a plain wooden mantle and built-in alcoves on either side occupied an entire facing wall. Rough-hewn logs were stacked to one side. Above the mantle rested a painting of cattle, similar to the ones Mayer had seen on his previous visit. Likely a commissioned piece.

A small corridor opened up just to the right of the fireplace wall. A staircase on his right led to what Mayer assumed were upper rooms. What passed for a kitchen rested against the left wall. It looked original to the house, before Lauck added on to the place. Vera stood by a pair of matching chairs that faced off a couch of opposing fabric; a coffee table acted as a referee between them. She wore a pink-and-white-striped, long-sleeve blouse, white slacks, and the kind of boots cowboys wore. The pink silk scarf wrapped around her neck was held in place, offset to the right, with a smart brooch; the long ends draped down the front of her blouse. The lobes of her ears were decorated with bright bobbles, and bearing down on the finger of her left hand—the one used to indicate wedded bliss—was the largest diamond ring Mayer had ever seen, one that likely weighed more than a small child. Alfried marking his territory for the world to see.

Cassi noticed the ranch's namesake as well.

"Come in, Mr. Mayer. I see you've brought a guest," Vera said.

Cassi stepped forward, not waiting for introductions. "Cassi Reyes, Mrs. Krupp. Very pleased to meet you." She extended a hand, one Vera took.

"What a pleasure to meet you as well," Vera said. "Please have a seat. I have read several of your articles in the paper. You have quite a way with words, my dear.

Cassi smiled and thanked her.

"I have coffee brewing on the stove. Or would you prefer tea?"

"Coffee's fine," Cassi said and took a seat on the couch.

Mayer took a seat next to her, though he turned his body to the side, uncomfortable with his back to the door. "I'll take tea," he said and placed his lid on the coffee table.

Cassi eyed the hat and wrinkled her nose. Mayer half expected to hear Diogie growl at him.

"Very well," Vera said and went to the kitchen. Once her back was turned, she added, "You may place your hat on the rack by the door."

Mayer rested the envelope on the couch next to Cassi then stood. He picked up his lid and hung it on one of the hooks of the coat rack, then went over to the corridor at the end of the fireplace wall. Just to the left of the staircase was an ornate grandfather clock, its pendulum swinging steadily to and fro. To the left of the clock was a portion of paneled wall and to the left still, an expansive built-in bookshelf filled mainly with photographs, knick-knacks, and a small number of books. Something about the space between the bookcase and the clock caught Mayer's attention. While the paneling matched that above the bookcase along the wall, something seemed out of place—a space wasted.

He stepped closer and was about to extend his hand to touch the wall, when one of the photographs on the bookshelf caught his attention. He picked it up for a closer look. There in the photo was Vera all dolled up in her wedding dress, Alfried by her side in a swallowtail tux. The couple was standing together, hand in hand, in a ridiculously elaborate room, all smiles. Behind them were shelves heavy with trinkets—plates, statues, awards, and the like—and on one of the shelves, just above Vera's left shoulder, resting on some type of stand, was the Seal of the Seven Archangels.

27

VERA RETURNED WITH a tray on which were set three flower-themed cups with saucers, a bowl of sugar, and a matching creamer. She laid the tray down on the coffee table and offered one of the cups to Cassi. "Coming, Mr. Mayer?" she asked.

Trying to appear as casual as possible, Mayer quickly returned the photo to the shelf, and rejoined the group, taking his position on the couch. Vera handed him the cup of tea; a metal chain hooked to the handle. He assumed an infuser was connected to the other end and wondered if, like Theo, Vera intended to read the leaves.

"Please help yourself to sugar and cream," Vera said, motioning to the tray. She took the remaining cup of coffee, along with two sugars, cream, and the chair in front of Mayer, crossing her legs as women do. "It seems you're a man who cannot be trusted," she said, giving the coffee a polite stir.

"I was just . . ."

"We agreed you'd come back to speak with Bessa, my housekeeper," Vera said, cutting him off. "You were supposed to come yesterday. You were expected."

"I was detained," Mayer said.

Vera pursed her lips. "I imagine you were," she said, then motioned to his face, pointing at it with the spoon and making a small circle. "This have something to do with your detainment?"

"Something," Mayer said.

"I suppose you'd like to speak to her now?" She placed the spoon on the saucer, and raised the cup to her pink lips.

"If I could."

"I'm afraid that's impossible," Vera said, with more than a hint of smugness. "She suffered an unfortunate incident and I gave her the week off."

"Incident?" Mayer questioned.

"She was dusting the very bookshelf with the photo you were just admiring when she fell from the stool, poor dear. Injured her arm and neck. I watched the whole thing happen. I can't tell you how many times I've told her to leave those top books be, but she was determined. She wanted to keep working even after the accident, but

I told her she needed to rest. A fall like that at her age, she could have broken a hip."

"Oh, my," Cassi said.

"When did this happen?" Mayer asked.

"The day you were supposed to call."

Vera sipped her coffee, holding herself like the actress she once was, patiently waiting for Mayer to make the next move. "And yet, you still agreed to see us," Mayer said.

"Call me intrigued. Something tells me there's more to all of this than your desire to question my housekeeper. Had that been a top priority, a man like you would've found a way to keep the appointment." She took another deliberate sip of coffee, then looked at Mayer intently. "Let's not let's pretend, Mr. Mayer. Why don't you just tell me why you're really here?"

Mayer placed the cup and saucer on the coffee table and retrieved the envelope he'd taken from Pierce's house. "Maybe you'd like to explain these." He opened the flap and poured the contents out onto the table.

Vera leaned forward and eyed the photographs. "How did you come across these?" she asked, coldly.

"Found them in Pierce's desk," Mayer said. "I was hoping you could tell me how they got there and what you were doing with the very man who's project you were trying to stop."

Vera glanced at the photos as casually as she would an advertisement for tissue paper, but Mayer knew better. He watched as her eyes darted from photo to photo, biting her lower lip, then bringing the cup to her mouth to buy time as she devised an appropriately clever response. Having attained a certain stature in life, Vera Krupp wasn't a woman used to being questioned, never mind being caught off guard—especially by the likes of Mayer.

He waited.

Vera uncrossed her legs and placed her cup and saucer on the table next to the photographs. She picked one up and examined it closely. "These photographs have been taken from a distance," she said. "No doubt by a person of unscrupulous character." She looked up at Mayer. "Perhaps a private detective, such as yourself."

Mayer let the slight pass and reached into the inside pocket of his coat, producing the cigarette case. He placed it on the coffee table.

Vera's eyes widened. "Where did you get that?" she asked quickly, then, realizing herself, regained her composure. "It's quite unique," she added, casually. "Very decorative."

"Boy," Mayer said, "you're good. I can see why you did so well in pictures. The only problem is, geliebte, I know where this particular cigarette case came from, or should I say I'm pretty sure I know *who* it came from."

Vera's face turned serious. "You're an interesting man, Mr. Mayer. I'll give you that. What is it you intend to do with these photos?"

"Me? Nothing. I just want the lowdown. What was going on between you and Hawthorne and why did it bother Pierce so much that he hired a private peeper?"

"How should I know?" Vera said.

"If not you, then who?" Mayer countered.

Vera remained stoic. She leaned back in the chair and recrossed her legs, then rested her hands gently on her lap, giving no hint to the truth. But Mayer was determined. "Why don't you start at the beginning," he said. "With you and Hawthorne."

"All right," Vera said. "Richard and I were seeing each other, there's no crime in that. He was single and I had already filed for divorce—though my marriage had ended long before I met Richard. We're both consenting adults."

"On opposite sides."

Vera brushed the fingers of one hand lightly across her lips. "Yes," she said. "I did not agree with his project and I tried to get him to stop."

"By pitching woo to him?"

"Mayer!" Cassi exclaimed. "That is completely uncalled for. You apologize right now."

Vera held up a hand. "Men like him don't apologize, my dear," Vera said to Cassi. "They mistakenly believe crassness is part of their charm. A man like Mr. Mayer here will always believe that the only weapon a woman possesses to influence a man is her body."

Mayer ignored the two women. "Listen sister, maybe I'm not pulling a full wagon, but these two men put more than a hundred thousand dollars into their project, and you expect me to believe that everything was wine and roses between you two and that the project, which you took him to court over, didn't put a crowbar in your relationship? It's time to get square, Mrs. Krupp. Two men are dead, two others almost lost their lives, and you seem to be right in the thick of things."

Vera took a deep breath, then exhaled slowly, as she straightened a shirt cuff that didn't need straightening. "Very well, Mr. Mayer," she began. "It was the project which brought us together and it was the project that split us apart. When they were just starting out, I invited both Richard and Mr. Pierce over to the ranch, with the hopes of helping them to understand that while the land was available, it was sacred and had been stolen from the local Paiutes and they should not build upon it."

"And how did that go?"

"Not well," Vera admitted. "So I tried a different tactic. I invited each man over separately to a private meal."

"Divide and conquer?"

Vera smiled.

"Didn't you think they'd tell each other?" Cassi asked.

"My dear, men are not that bright. When they see something they want, they keep it to themselves." She turned back to Mayer. "It was my intent to persuade, Mr. Mayer. Nothing else."

"But it didn't pan out that way, did it?"

"No. I guess it didn't. Richard would come to the ranch after work and sometimes we would ride; other times we would just sit and talk. We'd have a meal, then he would leave."

Mayer raised an eyebrow.

"You can lower your brow, Mr. Mayer. Holding hands, talking, and an occasional kiss is as far as it went. Not that it's any of your business. Richard and I had a great deal in common. I enjoyed his company and, I guess, I hoped that over time he would see things my way."

"And did he?"

Vera looked at the floor and straightened her cuff once again. "No, he didn't," she said softly, then looking up at Mayer added, "You are correct. My court proceeding did place a strain on our relationship."

"That why he offed himself?"

Vera's face tightened. "I assure you I was just as surprised at his suicide as anyone else. He gave no indication to me that . . ."

She didn't finish her sentence.

"Do you have any idea why he would leave you his part of the project?" Cassi asked.

Vera shook her head.

"And you gave him this cigarette case?" Mayer asked.

Vera admitted that she did and as she told the story, it began to click in Mayer's head. Why Pierce had hired a man to tail them. Why he had spoken so poorly of Hawthorne. The significance of the cigarette case and why it had been so important to both Hawthorne and Pierce—so much so that Pierce could not bear to see it destroyed. Then the ghostly echo suddenly came back to him, "I know what you did, William, and I know why you did it."

"Pierce was in love with you," Mayer said.

The statement caught both women off guard. "Excuse me?" Vera said.

"Pierce was in love with you, but it was unrequited love. Wasn't it?"

Vera brought her hand to her mouth. It was the first time Mayer had seen her nervous. He remained quiet, allowing that nervousness to fester until a stale stillness filled the house, one that proved too much for Vera to handle. "Do we have to do this, Mr. Mayer?"

"He made a pass at you, didn't he?"

Vera's eyes turned to steel. "Yes, Mr. Mayer, he did. Is that what you want to hear? Mr. Pierce made a pass at me, one that was not returned, I assure you."

"But he didn't take it well, did he? He wouldn't let it go."

Vera shook her head, slowly. "No, he wouldn't. I had to threaten him with the sheriff."

"So why did you go see him the other night?"

Vera looked genuinely surprised. "I'm sure I don't know what you're talking about."

"You didn't go over to his house and tell him you were going to donate your portion of the project to the Paiute Tribal Council?"

"I certainly did not!" Vera said, forcefully. "Quite the contrary, he came to the ranch trying to talk me out of stopping the project all together. I informed him it was my intent to donate my portion and ordered him off my ranch."

"Why would you do that?" Mayer asked. "Donate your portion of the project, I mean? What's in it for you?"

"Is that how you think, Mr. Mayer, only about what there is to gain from something? Only about how an action can benefit you? As if you're the only one that matters?"

"It's been my experience everyone thinks that way."

"And no one does anything just for the good of it? It's not possible for me to simply want to protect land sacred to another group of people?"

"Oh, it's possible," Mayer said, "but I don't see it. If you wanted to protect the land, why didn't you just buy it outright in the first place? There's enough sugar on that finger alone to buy half the county."

Vera gave Mayer cold eyes and a tight mouth to go with it, and, for a moment, he thought he might suffer the same fate his client had when he last came to the ranch. But then the lips relaxed and the eyes went back to cordial.

"The land was not for sale when Pierce and Richard bought it. They talked the owner into selling and the deal was done before anyone could intervene."

"Interesting," Mayer said. "Then why didn't you offer to buy out either man's share?"

Vera smiled. "Aren't you the clever one?"

With that, Mayer understood that Vera Krupp had indeed tried to buy them out, but it didn't take, which was likely why she switched tactics. "I only have one more question, Mrs. Krupp," Mayer said. "May I use your phone?"

28

MAYER PICKED UP the receiver and dialed. After three or four rings, the shaman answered. "I've got Cassi with me," Mayer said. "Mind if we come out to your place? I need to speak to Pierce."

"You're welcome to come, but Pierce is no longer here.

"What do you mean Pierce is no longer there?"

"He called for a car this morning and left."

"And you let him go?"

"He's not a prisoner, Mayer. I told him it was ill-advised to go until we got the situation under control. He wanted to leave and there's not much I could do about it."

"Dandy," Mayer said, more than a little frustrated. "Cassi and I will be at your place in less than an hour." After he hung up, Mayer returned to the sitting area, where Cassi and Vera were making polite conversation. He collected the photographs, returned them to the envelope, then slipped the cigarette case back into the inside pocket of his suit.

"Thank you for your time, Mrs. Krupp," Mayer said. "But we must be on our way."

Vera stood. "I don't suppose you could leave those here?"

"I'm sorry, I can't do that just yet."

Vera folded her arms across her chest and said curtly, "Well, I hope you found what you came for, Mr. Mayer."

"We'll see," Mayer said. He turned to the door and motioned for Cassi to follow him, retrieving his lid along the way. Cassi thanked Vera for her hospitality, then followed Mayer out the door. They were halfway down the walkway when Mayer stopped and turned. He stood, staring intently at the right side of the house. The stairs on the inside would have led to rooms upstairs, but the building was large enough that there should have been rooms downstairs as well, yet there was no door leading to those rooms that Mayer could see. No door on the inside or the outside.

"What is it?" Cassi asked.

"Nothing," Mayer said. "Let's go."

When Mayer got to the end of the dirt road, he turned and headed north, the escarpment spreading out on his side of the car. The trip to Vera Krupp's place had left him with a pit in his stomach. One mystery was coming together, while the other . . . well, the other still had a ways to go. Mayer wondered where the photograph he found on the shelf had been taken. A house, likely, but not just any house—an elaborate, fancy, expensive house. Alfried Krupp's house. If he was indeed in possession of the amulet, where was it now, and why did his bride, all the way in America, have a part of her house with no visible means of entry? *What*, he wondered, *was Vera Krupp hiding?*

"Where are we going?" asked Cassi.

"Pierce's house," Mayer said.

"I thought he was with the shaman."

"He was, but apparently he decided to leave sometime this morning. The man's a fool."

Fifteen minutes later, they were parked in front of Pierce's home. Mayer looked at the upstairs window. It was still broken out. "Wait here," he said to Cassi. It's not that Mayer expected Pierce to be at the house, but he needed to rule it out before he continued, so he slipped out of the Hornet, went to the door, and rang the bell. As he suspected, there was no answer. He tried twice more, and after still receiving no answer, returned to his car.

"Now where?" Cassi asked as he got behind the wheel.

"Shaman Mahkah's house."

A HALF HOUR passed before they arrived at the shaman's home. Mayer got out and headed to the back of the Hornet. Cassi followed. He opened the trunk, pulled out the Colt, popped the cylinder open, and, seeing that it was loaded, snapped it closed.

"You really think you're gonna need that?" Cassi asked.

"Can't be too sure," Mayer said putting the weapon back in its holster. "The witch has already attacked here once."

"Yes, but the elders helped the shaman place some type of blessing on the home and property. Shaman Mahkah said the skinwalker couldn't get near the place."

"Better not to take chances," Mayer said and closed the trunk.

Cassi sighed, then followed Mayer to the shaman's front door.

Shaman Mahkah let them in, shaking Mayer's hand and giving Cassi a hug. Diogie came over to Cassi, tail wagging, then turned and growled at Mayer. He would have a scar, but it looked to Mayer as if his wounds were healing nicely.

Mayer pulled the cigarette case from his pocket and tossed it to the shaman. "You wasted your time."

The shaman caught the case. "Oh, why do you say that?"

"I don't think it's the case that's drawing the ghost at all." Mayer filled the shaman in on the events of the previous night, including the photographs he found of Hawthorne and Krupp. Then he reviewed all the places the cigarette case had been with no appearance of the ghost. "Including Atomic Liquors, where I first met Pierce," Mayer said. "He pulled a cigarette from that very case when he was there. I didn't think anything of it at the time. But the case has made an appearance at too many places without Hawthorne's ghost in tow. Just to be sure, I kept it in my apartment last night."

"And the ghost did not come?"

"Nope."

"And you haven't seen it since?"

"Not even a shiver."

The shaman walked over to his table of herbs and laid the case down. "Then your supposition is correct," he said. "If it was attached to the object, it could have attacked you at any time, and yet, it did not."

"If it's not attached to the case, then what is it attached to?" Cassi asked.

"The house," Mayer said, flatly.

The shaman nodded his agreement. "There is something in that home that calls the spirit from the grave."

"So now what?" Cassi asked.

"Perhaps we should locate Pierce," the shaman suggested.

"How are we going to do that?" asked Cassi. "We already stopped by his house and he wasn't there."

"I think I know where he might be," Mayer offered.

The shaman gave Mayer a strange look. "Do you think we'll find the skinwalker in the same place?" he asked.

Mayer nodded.

"Then I had better prepare."

Mayer and Cassi waited while the shaman changed into ceremonial clothing. Mayer remained by the door. A blessing may have been placed on the house and the surrounding area, but Mayer was far more familiar with black magic than any man should be and understood all too well its life-threatening power. He wasn't about to take any chances.

Cassi rubbed Diogie between the ears. The dog showed its appreciation, while keeping one eye on Mayer at all times. The events of the past three days ran through Mayer's head—Pierce coming to the bar, the crime scene, Vera Krupp. Pieces of a puzzle all sliding into position, painting a gruesome and deadly picture. A love triangle with a skinwalker right smack dab in the middle. And the biggest question—the one Mayer didn't quite have worked out—was who, if anyone, was behind the witch, pulling the strings?

When the shaman returned, his face and hands were coated with a reddish-white ash, making him look more ghostlike than human. In his hands was a bowl filled with the same substance.

"You fall into a fire pit?" Mayer asked.

"Cedar ash. It will help protect against the witch. You should put on some as well."

Mayer was hesitant, but he knew that in times like these, it was better to listen to the experts—it was the same reason he had the rosary and the onyx around his wrists. He took the bowl and began applying the substance.

Cassi rolled her eyes, but did so as well.

"Could have used this the other night," Mayer said. "Or at the cave."

"To be quite frank," the shaman said. "I didn't really expect to find anything at the cave."

"Not sure I did either," Mayer admitted.

"I didn't know about the ash until the Navajo elder I told you about called me back," the shaman said, looking doleful. "Though I should have, since we dipped the bullets in ash."

"It's all right," Cassi said.

"Have you put it all together yet?" the shaman asked Mayer.

"I might have," Mayer said.

"What?" Cassi exclaimed. "You know what's going on and you haven't shared it with anyone?"

"I don't know that I'm right," Mayer said. "But if I am, we haven't much time."

"Then we better get going," the shaman said, taking hold of the ceremonial staff. "If you have anything else to tell me, you can do so in the car."

Mayer reached for the door, then stopped. "You sure you're up for this?" he asked the shaman. "I mean, with all you've been through. It could get gashouse."

"I'm ready," the shaman assured him.

Mayer turned and opened the front door and as he did, a pair of hands, cold as the grave, locked tightly around his neck. Instincts took over. Mayer grabbed icy arms and tried to twist them outward, but whatever had hold of his neck was far too strong. Darkness formed quickly around Mayer's eyes as he fought to stay conscious.

The man—yes it was a man—clutching his neck was missing most of the side of his head. But what caught Mayer's attention the most was his face—a look frozen in the terrified grip of sudden death. Mayer had seen the look and the face that beheld it once before—on a slab at the morgue. It was Hawthorne, but not in ghost form. This man was flesh and blood.

Mayer balled his fists and slammed them down hard onto Hawthorne's arms, but it did no good. He tried the technique again from underneath with the same results. And as the breath was squeezed from him, Mayer could feel his face flush with color, his head felt light, and within seconds he was unable to make a sound.

He thought he heard Cassi scream.

Diogie shot over and took hold of the man's leg and began violently shaking his head.

The shaman began chanting, "Kwaddü üü tühiwipü."

Mayer tried kicking Hawthorne in the shins and knees, but nothing seemed to help. Then he remembered the gun. He pulled the Colt from the holster and fired three times into Hawthorne's chest. The bullets shot through the man, slamming into the wall behind him. Mayer held the gun up to Hawthorne's head and tried again, but met with the same results. He took the barrel of his piece and slammed it against what was left of Hawthorne's head—over and over again—as hard as he could. Thud, thud, thud. And as the darkness took over, and Mayer's body fell limp, he thought he saw his mother standing by the door, arms outstretched.

29

MAYER AWOKE TO find himself splayed out on the floor. Cassi was kneeling by him on one side, the shaman on the other, holding something pungent under Mayer's nose. Diogie was at his feet with a look that Mayer could have sworn was concern.

"Thought we lost you there," the shaman said.

"You and me both," Mayer replied. He went to sit upright and made it as far as his elbow before the hammering in his head stopped him. Shaman Mahkah took him by the forearm and helped him the rest of the way.

"Sit here for a moment while I make you something to drink," the shaman said.

"If it's that cactus tea, I'll pass."

The shaman ignored him.

"Are you all right?" Cassi asked, her face steeped in concern.

"I'm right as the mail," Mayer lied, rubbing his temple. After a moment the fuzziness in his head began to dissipate and he could see that Hawthorne's lifeless body was lying motionless on the floor next to him. Mayer also noticed something he had missed before. Hawthorne was completely naked. "Well ain't that a bite," he said.

The shaman returned with a cup of hot liquid. "Drink this," he said. "Slowly."

Mayer brought the drink to his nose. The dark liquid smelled like turpentine. "You trying to poison me?" he asked.

"If I wanted you dead, I would have let this man here finish his task," he said, motioning to the body with his head.

"What stopped him?" Mayer asked and took a sip. The liquid tasted worse than it smelled and it showed on Mayer's face.

"The shaman," Cassi said. "He just kept chanting and suddenly it dropped to the floor. And not a minute too soon!"

"I just encouraged the body to return to the grave from whence it came."

"Except it didn't come from any grave," Mayer said. "The witch stole it from the coroner's slab." He took another sip at the shaman's encouragement, wrinkling his face again in the process. "How did it get in here?" he asked. "I thought you blessed the place."

"Against the living," the shaman said. "Not the dead. The skinwalker could not get in, so he must have sent Hawthorne in his steed."

"Talk about the perfect hatchet man," Mayer said. "How d'ya charge a stiff with murder, especially when he's already been chilled off?"

After several minutes Mayer was able to stand without seeing stars. The shaman made him choke down another cup of the black liquid, and when he was done, the three of them stood in a circle looking down at the body.

Cassi wrapped her arms around herself and gave the body a sneer. "Can't we cover him?"

"Which part?" Mayer asked, and it was then that he noticed the forefinger on Hawthorne's right hand was missing.

"So that's how the witch did it," Mayer said.

"Did what?" Cassi asked.

"Got Hawthorne's ghost to haunt Pierce in his home. She must have cut off the finger and placed it in the home somehow."

"Now how could she do that?" Cassi asked. "Besides, you don't know that he wasn't just missing the finger. Maybe he lost it in the war."

"Hard to pull a trigger with no forefinger," Mayer said. "Plus there was nothing in the coroner's report about a missing finger."

"Do you want to call the police?" the shaman asked.

Mayer rubbed his cheek. "I'd rather just take care of the body here," he said. "That going to be a problem?"

The shaman shook his head. "Best to get rid of black magic when it appears. Bring the body outside. I'll prepare the fuel."

Mayer bent down and took hold of Hawthorne's arm at the shoulder. Then he squatted, pulled Hawthorne's dead body up and onto his back. He struggled at first, but managed to get to his feet and carry the body outside. He took it far enough away to ensure the odor of burning flesh wouldn't permeate the shaman's home.

When the shaman arrived with the fuel, Mayer suggested that Cassi might want to wait inside the home with Diogie. "It's not a pleasant smell or a pleasant sight," he said.

"I'll go with you," the shaman said to Cassi. "It is not something I wish to see either." He turned to Mayer. "Be careful with that. It is a mixture of my own that will definitely reduce the body to ash."

Mayer nodded, wondering just exactly what the shaman had put in the fuel and why a healer would know how to disappear a stiff. He reasoned it was probably best not to ask.

After everyone left, Mayer went to his car. He placed his suit coat inside and took out a handkerchief, which he tied loosely around his neck. Then he returned to the body, built a small pyre, and laid Hawthorne on top. After applying a generous helping of the shaman's fuel on everything, Mayer, lit the pyre, and stepped back as it burst into flames. He pulled the handkerchief up over his mouth and nose, as dark smoke filled the air and sparks shot upward, releasing the black magic.

WHEN IT WAS all said and done, Mayer returned the handkerchief and retrieved his suit coat, then he went back into the house. There he found Shaman Mahkah, Diogie at his feet, and Cassi sitting and drinking tea like a couple of sophisticates.

The shaman looked to Mayer. "Is it done?"

Mayer nodded. He was about to ask if anyone knew the whereabouts of his Colt and lid, when he saw them resting on the end table next to the shaman's chair.

"I've been catching up Shaman Mahkah on what I found about the skinwalker," Cassi said.

"And?" Mayer asked as he moved over to the end table.

"It is interesting." The shaman placed his cup on the table to his left and stood. "And you believe this woman, Hak'az Asdzą́ą́ is the skinwalker?" he asked, pronouncing the name much different than either Mayer or Cassi had.

"I think it's a good bet," Cassi said.

"Right now it's the only bet," Mayer added. "Besides, Cassi could find no other record of a killing on Navajo land that would lead to the Paiutes in any way."

"I'm not sure I agree that a skinwalker would protect sacred land," the shaman said, "especially land sacred to another tribe."

"That was my concern as well," Mayer admitted.

The shaman rubbed his cheek thoughtfully, as one would when searching for holes in reasoning. Having found none, he said, "The dates do seem right." He looked to Mayer, "but when the time comes, you'd better let me pronounce the name."

Mayer chuckled.

"I suggest we get going," Cassi said.

Mayer picked up the Colt and put it where it belonged. "Let's go," he said, donned his lid, and went to the front door. Cassi and the shaman followed. This time when Mayer opened it, he did so slowly, using the door itself as a shield. It wasn't that he really expected anything to be there, he just thought, after all that happened, it was best to be cautious.

They took Mayer's car and headed toward town. As the trio drove down the road, one thought bounced around in Mayer's head. It was something that had been pestering him like a frayed thread on the arm of a suit coat—something he couldn't make work out. Why had Pierce left the protection of the shaman's home? The man had been attacked by the very thing that sent his partner to the great beyond, yet he left the one place where he was likely the safest. It didn't fit. Unless, of course, Pierce wasn't really afraid of the outcome, wasn't truly worried about being attacked. But if Mayer was right—and he was pretty sure he was—Pierce was operating from the wrong side of the boat.

Pierce would've had the time to go back to his own home by now and, seeing the damage, would likely have put two and two together. But it wasn't to Pierce's house that they were heading. No, Cassi's research and their little talk with Vera Krupp had begun to help put all the pieces in order. Words can be used as misdirection, lies delivered with a steady tongue. But the body did not always go along with the fancy line of gab. Unconscious moments—the straightening of a shirt cuff that didn't need straightening, the biting of a lip, a certain placement of the hands—could betray the liar, without her even knowing. Over the years, Mayer had learned to trust the body, not the words.

Vera did everything she could to try and stop the pair from building on that sacred land. When she couldn't buy them out and playing nice didn't work, she used her substantial influence to bring the law into play. And when even that didn't work, she tried something else—something primal. Something that drove a wedge between the partners. And whether there were real feelings beyond protecting the land on her part or not, it had definitely worked. Mayer wasn't sure he believed her story about Pierce making an unwelcomed pass. He thought it more likely the pass was not only welcomed, but sought after. Then, once achieved, all it took was a hint, a batting of the eyes, a proposal to keep the affair a private matter so as not to worry the other partner.

Both men bit.

Then it was a simple matter of rejecting one and keeping on with the other. A gift—perhaps a cigarette case—one that could be used in the open without worry, but would definitely catch the attention of just the right man. A secret message inside, a word known to both men, awoke the green-eyed monster. Mayer had to admit, she had played the part well—an actress to the very end.

Still, there was the suicide and the suicide note. Hawthorne had definitely killed himself, and he had definitely written the note. And while it was clear the skinwalker was the one who made Hawthorne write the note, then send himself to the big sleep against his will, what Mayer didn't know was why. It was something he was about to find out as the trio bounced down the dirt road toward the trailer. And when they arrived, Mayer was not at all surprised to find Pierce's Cadillac parked outside.

30

MAYER STOPPED THE car a short distance from the trailer, not wanting Pierce to hear their approach. He cautioned his companions not to slam the doors, then reloaded the Colt before exiting the car.

"Ready?" he asked.

Cassi and the shaman both nodded and followed Mayer step per step to the trailer. They were but a few steps away when they heard two unpleasantly loud voices coming from inside.

"That was not our agreement!" the male voice exclaimed. It was one both Mayer and the shaman recognized immediately.

"I did what you asked me to do," said the other voice. It was low and gravelly, yet calm. Mayer had to strain to hear it.

"Did you?" Pierce yelled back. "Since when did we agree to R. J. signing over his portion of the project to that kraut? Do you have any idea what that will has done to me? If she turns that property over to the tribe, I'll be ruined."

Mayer thought he heard laughing in response. But it wasn't the lighthearted kind heard at a dinner party or in a theater. No, this laugh was menacing.

"Oh, you find that funny do you?"

The laughing continued, echoing out into the escarpment.

"And my man," Pierce said. "That wasn't part of the deal either. And what was that . . . thing that came crashing through my window? That was you, wasn't it?" he demanded. "None of this was part of the plan!"

"Why did you hire the tattooed man? You ask me to solve your problem, I do as you ask, then you turn on me?"

"*Me* ask *you*?" Pierce said incredulously. "You came to me and offered to take care of the problem. You're the one who told me R. J. was seeing Vera—my Vera. It was all your idea. And it was you, not me, who complicated things."

"But it was you who agreed to it all. What did you think was going to happen?"

"You're a witch!"

There was a silence. Then Pierce spoke again, "You've complicated things for the final time."

"What do you plan to do with that?"

"Get rid of loose ends."

Mayer didn't wait another minute. He rushed through the door, hitting it with his shoulder and slamming it hard against the wall. The two occupants inside turned and stared—eyes wide. Pierce was still dressed in the same clothing he'd been in when Mayer left him at the shaman's house the night before. He looked worn, angry, and in need of a good shave—his hand whiteknuckled the handle of a pistol.

The elderly woman with him was stocky enough to hold her own. Her round face was etched with the scars of life, only hers were deeper, much more pronounced. They twisted her face into a grotesque form that barely resembled that of a human. And, buried deep inside the folds, were the yellow eyes of a coyote—eyes Mayer had seen once before, when they were accompanied by the voice of his long-lost mother. Only this time the woman wasn't naked. This time she was clothed in the uniform of a housekeeper.

She didn't stay that way for long.

As the skinwalker let out a stream of words Mayer did not understand, the air inside the trailer grew heavy, thick with darkness. She ripped off her uniform and threw it to the ground—her body, like before, naked, except for the covering of ceremonial symbols.

It was at that moment that Mayer knew his suspicions had been correct. The housekeeper had been the key to it all. She had worked for Krupp and for Hawthorne, and she had worked for Pierce. In fact, she was the reason his house was so clean. She also happened to be a skinwalker. Mayer was about to pull the Colt when he remembered the luck he'd had previously and decided to leave it holstered.

The shaman appeared, Cassi close behind. He raised his arms to the sky, the staff in hand. Then he threw something powdery at the witch and started chanting. The skinwalker turned all her attention to him. They began parrying word for word. Sparks flew from fingertips and the air clashed with thunder.

Pierce tried to run, but Mayer caught him by the shirt collar and slapped the gun from his hand. "Going somewhere?" he asked. "Someone else need killing?"

Pierce grew defiant. "Well aren't you the smart one?" he said. "Got it all figured out, don't you?"

"Sure," Mayer said. "You left the suitcase for me to find. You know, the one you filled with Hawthorne's clothes. And I took it from there, only, just like this little mess, it didn't work out the way you planned."

Suddenly the trailer rocked to one side, sending Pierce and Mayer crashing into the wall. Cassi took hold of the door frame. The shaman seemed fixed in position, as did the witch. Pierce took the opportunity to strike Mayer across the chin, but it was a marshmallow blow. The kind thrown by a man more used to handling money than fisticuffs. Mayer sent one back, only he knew how to make it stick.

The trailer lurched back to its original position, throwing Cassi inside the trailer. Mayer used the momentum to land another punch—one that knocked Pierce to the floor. Then he turned to the skinwalker and pulled out his Colt, figuring that if the witch was distracted, he might be able to get in a good shot.

That was when he heard them. Snarls coming from outside the trailer. He turned and saw three sets of yellow eyes attached to the teeth-baring faces of three coyotes. Cassi saw his look, turned, and screamed. It caught the shaman's attention and he turned as well. It was all the witch needed. She spoke the words and thrust her hands forward, propelling the shaman to the ground. Cassi ran to him.

Mayer stepped forward, balled his left hand into a fist, and hit the witch hard in the face. It did nothing but anger her more than she already was. She raised her hand to strike him and as she did, Mayer pulled up his sleeve and exposed his tattoo. As before, it froze the witch in her tracks, and just as Mayer moved to strike her again, the coyotes leapt in front of the witch, forcing him backward.

Mayer lifted the Colt and took aim at the skinwalker's neck, but just as he pulled the trigger, he was attacked from behind. Pierce had found some semblance of courage and began striking Mayer. The bullet hit high and to the right of the skinwalker's head. It was enough to pop her out of the trance the tattoo had placed her in. Mayer turned and backhanded Pierce, sending him over the desk and onto the floor. He turned back to the skinwalker and raised the weapon, just as she dashed out the trailer door.

Mayer fired, not knowing if the bullet found its mark, then he turned on Pierce. The man had recovered and was inching his way to the door as well. Mayer took aim.

"Where do you think you're going?"

"What are you going to do, Mr. Mayer?" Pierce said. "Shoot an unarmed man?"

Mayer thought hard about it for a moment, weighing his options, then Cassi called out his name. "We've got bigger problems here!" she exclaimed.

Mayer had forgotten about the coyotes. They were still there, teeth baring, creating a barrier between them and the exit. Worse yet, now that the witch was gone, they were beginning a slow advance. Mayer moved the gun from Pierce to the animals.

"No!" the shaman called out. "They are in a trance, controlled by the witch."

"Well, if you've got a better idea, now's the time!"

The shaman spoke, as he had done before, in words foreign to Mayer. Then he took a little bit of the powder he had with him, held up the palm of his hand and blew. The powder turned to a crystal blue smoke that snaked its way toward the coyotes. The slow, slithering movement captivated them. They watched as the smoke drew closer and closer, then suddenly split into thirds and entered the nostrils of all three animals. The coyotes blinked quickly and threw their heads back, as if they had just been given smelling salts. They eyed the group, then escaped to the outside.

Mayer lowered his weapon.

Pierce regained his composure, brushed himself off, then scuttled away.

Cassi helped the shaman to his feet. "Quick," he said, "we need to get to that cave."

31

AFTER A STOP at the car to discard unnecessary items, such as suit coats and hats, the three scrambled up the side of the escarpment as fast as the terrain would permit. The shaman had not been injured in his scrape with the witch, though that was likely due to the timely revealing of Mayer's tattoo. Once they reached the ledge to the outside of the cave, they climbed up and peered into the darkness.

"I do not think the witch is here," the shaman said.

"How can you tell?" Mayer asked.

"I do not feel her presence."

"Then where could she be? She didn't have any pelts or feathers, so she couldn't transform. She'd need to come here to get them."

"What if she has them hidden somewhere else?" Cassi offered. "You know, in case she couldn't make it to the cave?"

It was a smart thought. Mayer was impressed.

"That could be," The shaman said. "But they would have to be hidden somewhere no one is likely to find them."

"Like in an abandoned building?" Mayer asked.

"Yes, that would work. So long as the witch had access to it."

"Vera told me the buildings which made up the early campsite still exist on the property," Mayer said. "The witch could come and go as she pleased without suspicion."

"Then we'd better get to that ranch," the shaman said.

"And what if she doubles back here?" Cassi asked.

"I can place a protection on the cave that will prevent her from being able to enter."

"Better do it quick," Mayer said. He waited impatiently, resisting the urge to run down the escarpment by himself, as the shaman drew a symbol in the dirt in front of the entrance to the cave with his staff, all the time chanting in what Mayer assumed was Paiute. When he finished, they headed down to the trailer. They fell once or twice in the process, but arrived in relatively one piece. They jumped into Mayer's car and headed to Vera's ranch.

They had no sooner pulled into the drive, when they saw Vera Krupp and her gatekeeper, Peg Westburg, running for their lives down the escarpment toward the ranch house. They were coming from the back of the property where the old buildings Vera had described still stood—the skinwalker hot on their trail. Mayer didn't wait. As they shot into Vera's front door, he leapt from the vehicle and ran toward the house. The shaman yelled for him to stop, but Mayer didn't listen. He heard a woman scream, threw open the front door, and rushed inside.

The skinwalker was there, transformed, coyote skins draped over her back and head. Peg Westburg was standing next to the witch, a chrome-plated six-shooter with a pearl handle in her hand. It was pointed at Vera Krupp. Even from this angle Mayer could see Peg was in a trance, controlled by the skinwalker.

"Hey, Bessa!" Mayer called out.

The skinwalker turned and in an instant leapt to the door. Mayer dove out of the way, rolling when he hit the floor. He pulled the Colt, pointed it in the direction of the skinwalker, and fired. The front window crashed with the impact of the bullet. The skinwalker turned and faced Mayer. It took a tentative step forward, then stopped and gripped its shoulder, as a yellow substance dripped down its arm.

Mayer smiled. While the shot hadn't met its mark, it had hit something—at least that was a start. He took aim and shot again, but the gun jammed. The skinwalker sprung toward Mayer, picked him up and tossed him hard into the bookcase, its contents crashing down around him. His Colt slid across the floor.

Cassi and the shaman came running in. Peg Westburg dropped the gun and collapsed. Vera ran for the weapon and snatched it from the floor.

The shaman spoke: "Hak'az Asdzą́ą́ you are a skinwalker." But it had no effect. Mayer didn't know who was more surprised, him, Cassi, or the shaman.

The skinwalker took quick action. It jumped at the shaman, grabbed him by the shirt, and tossed him through the broken window, all in one swift move. A shot was fired, then another, and another: each one hitting its mark and each one doing no good at all. Cassi fell to the floor, taking cover behind a chair. Vera emptied three more shots into the skinwalker, before it turned on her.

Mayer got to his knees and tried to catch his breath. He pulled up his sleeve to expose his tattoo, but the skinwalker was not looking at him. Instead, its eyes were locked with Vera's. He called out, "Bessa!" but the skinwalker did not turn. Vera's eyes were saucers as she brought the weapon to her head and cocked the hammer. Her pleading eyes locked with Mayer's.

"Do something, Mayer!" Cassi yelled.

Mayer struggled to collect his thoughts. *Why hadn't the name worked?* He was sure what Cassi had uncovered was the answer. Hak'az Asdzą́ą́ had to be a skinwalker. And then it hit him. This skinwalker's name wasn't Hak'az Asdzą́ą́, but he knew what it was.

"Thocmentony!" he yelled.

The witch turned to face him.

"You are a skinwalker!"

The witch's face twisted with pain and she began transforming, only this time it was involuntary. They all stood, transfixed by the savagery, as the witch fought the process—her face shifting from human to coyote and back again. The arms and legs doing the same, until it was impossible to tell if the thing was human or creature.

The witch let out a torturous cry, the pain unbearable. Or maybe it was her fate finally catching up with her. Either way, when it was all said and done the witch knelt on the floor, naked and sobbing.

Vera dropped her pistol.

Mayer picked his up. He walked over and stood above the witch. She glared up at him.

"This is not over," she said.

"You're mistaken," Mayer said and pointed the gun at her.

One last shot echoed through the canyons.

32

MAYER'S FIRST CALL was to Detective Fry. The incident was out of his jurisdiction, but Fry would know who to call. Luckily, Vera Krupp was deputized as well. Mayer also needed someone to pick up Pierce and take him in, and that was something Fry could do.

Peg Westburg had regained consciousness and was resting in a chair as the brown boys got to work. Cassi attended to the shaman. She had managed to set him upright against a post, and while he protested the calling of an ambulance, she was fairly sure his arm was broken and didn't know what other injuries he might have.

Vera Krupp stood against the fireplace with a look that was either shock or annoyance, Mayer couldn't tell. A portly man with a cheesy mustache and two bars on each of his brown collars spoke to her first and when finished came over to Mayer.

"I'm going to need that bean shooter," he said, smelling of coffee.

Mayer pulled it from the holster and offered it to the deputy. "So long as I get it back."

The deputy took the gun and looked it over. "This that new Colt?"

Mayer nodded.

He held it up, testing the weight, then tucked the barrel inside his duty belt. "You the one they call 'Night Mayer?'"

Mayer didn't answer.

"Fry says you were involved in the Sloan Canyon incident."

"I suppose I was."

He raised a single brow. "You as barmy as they say?"

Mayer let out a light chuckle.

"Seems like this ran along those lines."

Mayer nodded.

"Gonna put me behind the eight ball, you know?"

"I know."

He remained quiet for a moment, scraping his hand across his chin, then spoke: "Housekeeper goes crazy and tries to take out her employer. Luckily a stranger with a new Colt just happens by."

"Something like that."

The deputy let out a humph. "Guess I'll figure out something." He turned to leave, then stopped. "Call me in a couple days. Once ballistics comes back, I'll return your piece."

Mayer nodded and thanked the deputy. He walked across the room to where Vera was standing, alone, arms wrapped around herself. "You okay?" he asked.

She looked at him blankly.

"What happened?"

"Peg and I were walking the property, as we do weekly," Vera began. She rubbed her arms lightly as she spoke, "and Peg thought she saw someone go into one of the old buildings on the upper part of the property. I thought she might be seeing things, but she insisted, so we went to have look." She paused and stopped rubbing her arms. "She was naked, covered in . . . in markings of some kind. We surprised her, and then she . . ."

"Transformed?" Mayer offered.

Vera nodded and took to rubbing her arms again. "That . . . thing, was my housekeeper?"

Mayer told her it was.

"It was in my home all this time?"

"Yes, but I don't think it ever had any intention to hurt you. Not until . . . well, it all went south." Mayer explained to Vera how her affair with Hawthorne had led to Pierce hiring her housekeeper to kill the man. But the skinwalker, enjoying a good trick, had complicated matters and compelled Hawthorne to sign a will that turned Vera into an even greater wedge.

"Are you implying this was all my fault?" Vera asked. She tried to put forth a brave face, but the tears welling in her eyes betrayed her.

"I guess you're the only one who can answer that," Mayer said. "Only you know what was truly in your heart." He should have told her that the witch probably had plans to kill the partners anyway—to protect that land—and that Vera's part in the whole thing was likely minimal, but decided better of it. Pierce did what he did because of her and that was that.

"I was . . ." She paused. "I was only trying to protect land that was sacred to the Paiutes."

"It's your story, sister."

"You don't believe me, do you?"

"It's not up to me to believe. But I can't reckon why the Paiutes would be so important to you. You're not a member of their tribe."

"You don't have to be a member of a particular group to understand their plight, Mr. Mayer." Her voice softened. "You just have to witness it for yourself." She paused, then after a moment, found renewed strength. "Bessa, Buster, and I spoke often about the trials their people were forced to endure at the hands of white men. What it was like to be a stranger in your own land." Her eyes reflected a certain understanding, or perhaps it was compassion.

Mayer instantly thought of the Jews and the holocaust in Germany, and what a woman like Vera Krupp might have witnessed. He should have felt sorry for her, but he didn't. Love was just as strong as magic and when used the wrong way, it could turn just as black.

"You truly had no idea what she was?" Mayer asked.

"How would I?"

"The eyes. Didn't you notice the eyes?"

"Some people have strange eyes, Mr. Mayer. Hers were not the first I've seen that were yellow."

Mayer wondered where Vera Krupp could possibly have seen yellow eyes before, but decided to leave it alone. He was about to walk out when Vera asked him a question.

"What will you do with the photographs?"

Mayer looked at the women before him, seeing her helpless for likely the first time in her adult life. "Wait here," he said, then walked over to the shattered bookcase. He fished through the debris until he found the photograph he'd picked up before and brought it back to Vera Krupp.

"Where was this taken?" he asked, handing her the photo.

She examined it through the cracked glass. "This was at my husband's home," she said. "Why do you ask?"

"Do you recognize that amulet over your left shoulder?"

Vera took a second look. "I don't," she said. "Why? Is it important?"

"It's the Seal of the Seven Archangels," Mayer said.

Vera showed no recognition of the name.

"It's an amulet believed to hold extreme powers. Hitler was searching for it and there it sat on the shelf in your husband's home."

"I see," Vera said. "Yes, Mr. Mayer, I knew my husband was drawn to the occult. It was just one of the many things I learned about him after we were married— when it was far too late. I also discovered his connection to Hitler and the war machines. That is why I chose to come back to the states after the passing of my mother. It is also why I filed for divorce."

"One of those quickie deals?" Mayer asked. He shouldn't have said it, but did anyway.

Vera didn't answer.

"What are you hiding behind that bookcase?" Mayer asked.

Vera glanced in that direction. "I assure you, there is nothing there that would interest you."

Mayer gave her hard eyes and waited.

"Very well. Come with me," she said, and placed the photograph on the coffee table. She walked over to the space between the clock and the bookcase, touched the panel in a certain spot, and slid it open. "Go ahead," she said, moving aside.

Mayer stepped into one of the largest bedrooms he had ever seen. Decorated in multiple shades of pink with cream accents, it was complete with all the trappings of a regular bedroom, but also included a spacious sitting area with two pink, tufted chairs; a powder room with a lighted vanity; and a sunken tub large enough to invite a guest—or two.

"It's quite the setup," Mayer said.

"It's my little getaway," Vera explained. "When I don't want to be disturbed, I come here. The staff doesn't know about it, so they won't bother me. You are welcome to search the drawers and the closets if it will put your mind at ease, Mr. Mayer, but I assure you, I did not share my husband's fascination with the occult and I have nothing of his here. If that amulet was on the shelf of his home, then I imagine it is still there. Perhaps he would be open to showing it to you."

It didn't ring true. Alfried had already done his bit in the cooler by the time he and Vera married, so unless she was a fool, she knew about his war crimes long before she married him and pulled the pin anyway.

Still, what were the chances she would open a secret room for Mayer to search if the amulet were indeed there. She had her ranch and she had her rock, what more did she need?

"I'll take a rain check," Mayer said and left the room.

Vera closed the panel behind him. "And those photographs?" she asked.

Mayer shook his head. "Sorry, they're evidence now. It's out of my hands." He headed for the front door. "See you in the funny papers."

33

THE AMBULANCE TOOK the shaman away and Cassi with him. Mayer gave his statement and was free to leave, but admonished not to pull out of town—like he had somewhere to go. Truth be told, he did have one stop to make.

Pierce's home was dark when he arrived—the upstairs window still broken. He traded his Colt for an iron club and a container of salt, then went to the door. He twisted the knob, then threw his shoulder into the thing, popping the lock—grateful he hadn't latched the deadbolt. He stood inside the dark home for a moment, inches away from the blood that had surely made an indelible stain on the floor by now, and tried to figure out where the skinwalker would hide such a thing as a finger. He wished Diogie was there to sniff it out.

Though he had come prepared, Mayer was none too eager for another encounter with Hawthorne's ghost. He knew he didn't have time to search the entire house before it, once again, appeared. As much as Mayer enjoyed the dark, he knew it would be easier and more productive to search with the lights on, so he tripped the switch by the door and scanned the rooms—wondering where he'd put a finger if he was a skinwalker.

For no particular reason he could determine, Mayer was drawn to the living room. A place for everything and everything in its place. Shelves were full of trinkets and showroom figurines. A rectangular coffee table sat crosswise on a Persian rug and decorative pillows rested on the couch at each corner. *Perhaps*, Mayer thought, *the finger might be there in the cushions, among the spare change.*

That was when the fly entered the room, followed by another—imperfections in a masterpiece of cleanliness, certainly not acceptable at Goodalls or Harrods. He turned to the bloodstain and found them there—some landing on the blood, others hovering just above. He hadn't noticed them when he entered, but he should have. He should have heard them too. And now that he did, the buzzing was all he could hear. He thought of the trailer and the pool of dried blood on the desk. One of the flies broke from the crowd. Mayer followed it as it flew across the room and over to the mantle. It passed an elaborately decorated clock and lit atop a capped famille noire vase. It was a beautiful piece, displaying two colorful birds resting on a flowered branch—one male and one female. Other flies had found the vase as well.

"That's it," Mayer said. "A trickster to the end."

Mayer went to the vase, rested his club against the chair, and placed the container of salt on the mantle. Then he removed the lid. Almost immediately, he was overtaken with a smell so foul that it left no doubt as to the contents of the vase. He tilted it toward him and there, inside, he found the missing finger—purple, black, and beginning to rot. *How*, Mayer wondered, *did flies always know just where to find the goodies?*

He pulled out his handkerchief and took hold of the thing. He was about to toss it into the fireplace when Hawthorne's ghost appeared. This time Mayer was ready. He put down the finger, took hold of the salt container, and poured a measure into his hand. Then he tossed it squarely at the specter, making it quickly disappear. But Mayer knew it was only momentary, so before it could come back, he threw the digit into the fireplace, along with the handkerchief, doused it with lighter fluid, and lit the thing with the matches Pierce kept next to the hearth.

As it went ablaze, Mayer took hold of the club and waited. When the ghost appeared again, Mayer steadied himself, but as the finger burned to ashes, the ghost in front of him began to reflect the burning. The sparks started at the ghost's feet and made their way up the body, until there was nothing left.

Mayer took a deep breath then left the house and all that it represented. He climbed into the Hornet and let it ferry him home. Along the way, the events replayed in his head. Vera Krupp had gotten two men, two partners, and likely two friends, to land on opposite sides, by awakening the most dangerous of all the emotions—jealousy. Then she rubbed it in their faces. All the time the skinwalker made her plans. She took a job at Pierce's house and then one cleaning the office, where she could stay in the thick of things.

Then all she had to do was make an offer to a man dizzy with a dame—one who didn't return the favor. Maybe Pierce agreed right away or maybe he let it percolate a bit before taking action, but either way, act he did. And being a skinwalker, the witch couldn't help but throw a crowbar into the mix. Enter one suicide note.

The car stopped in front of Mayer's apartment and he got out. He donned his suit coat and lid and shut the door. He'd taken a couple steps toward his front door, when his gut twisted. Mayer knew he could only run so long before he'd have to bite the bullet, so he turned and headed inside Atomic Liquors.

Joe was tending bar. He smiled when Mayer entered, then nodded to a man seated at one of the stools who was smoking a cigarette and nursing a drink. It was Fry. Mayer went to the restroom to wash the ash from his face and hands, then headed to the oversized detective.

"What d'ya know, if it isn't our own little troublemaker?" Fry said when he saw Mayer.

"Can it, Fry," Mayer said. "You come here just to yank my chain?"

"That and tell you we caught your man."

"He say anything?"

Fry shook his head. "Lawyered up."

"Doesn't surprise me," Mayer said.

Fry gave Mayer the once over, then shook his head. "So you think Pierce hired this . . . skinwalker of yours to take out his partner?"

Mayer shook his head. "I don't think Pierce had any idea what he was hiring. When that thing jumped through his window, he was as scared as a rat in a pit of snakes. He had no clue what, or should I say who, it was. But I think he did know the housekeeper had some type of powers he could use to his advantage."

Fry nodded his understanding and blew out a thick cloud of smoke.

Mayer continued. "Once he discovered his partner was two-timing him with the woman he loved, Pierce lost his head. Krupp's housekeeper, Bessa, managed to squirm her way into all their lives and was the only one who knew the story from all three angles. Heck, Hawthorne probably didn't even know Pierce had hired her to clean his house."

Joe slid a glass in front of Mayer. He didn't have to taste it to know it was rum. He took a snort. "She must have offered to take care of the problem and Pierce . . . well, Pierce didn't ask how. Then she hoodwinked him and Pierce tried to take her out—finally understanding that she was the skinwalker."

"Slow learner," Fry said.

"Indeed," Mayer agreed.

Fry took a drink. "When did you suspect your boss was making you out for a rube?" Fry asked. It was what Mayer liked most about the man. Fry hadn't asked him if he knew he was being played for a patsy, he just assumed Mayer had it figured from the get-go.

Mayer grinned. "When I saw his hired man at the trailer. If you suspected your partner was murdered, enough to hire a man who goes strapped to protect your own self, why would you go anywhere without that man? Pierce came to me in the bar alone. That's not the actions of a man worried about being next in line."

"A wrong number from the start, eh?"

Mayer agreed.

Fry stood and crushed his cigarette into the ashtray on the bar. "Don't worry, kid, we should have enough to make it stick. Maybe even an electric cure."

"Dandy," Mayer said.

Fry's face changed to one of concern. "You okay kid? You look like you've been through one."

"I'll make it out all right."

Fry wasn't convinced and it showed. He downed the rest of his drink, then replaced his lid. He laid a strong hand on Mayer's shoulder, nodded, then left without saying a word.

After Fry left, Mayer eyed an empty table in the corner, took his glass there, and waited for Stella to join him. He had a dress-down coming and he knew it.

The glass was almost empty when Cassi strolled into the bar, the shaman at her side—his arm in a cast. Joe saw them too. He looked to Mayer and received permission in the form of a nod. He pointed to Mayer's table and they came over.

"Mind if we sit?" she asked.

Mayer motioned to the chairs. "How's the arm?" he asked the shaman.

"Much ado about nothing," he replied.

"Minor concussion and a broken arm is hardly nothing," Cassi offered, but admitted Shaman Mahkah probably knew more about healing than anyone in the hospital.

Mayer smiled. Joe came to the table, filled Mayer's glass, and took Cassi's and the shaman's order.

"I doubt they have cactus tea here," Mayer said.

Joe twisted his face. "We don't," he confirmed.

"What I'd like to have is a boulevardier," the shaman said. "But I'd better stick to tea."

Cassi ordered an old fashioned.

When Joe left, the shaman addressed Mayer, "You didn't have to shoot her, you know. She would have died on her own in three days."

Mayer cupped his hands around his glass. "Why take the chance?" he said, without looking up.

"How did you know?" Cassi asked.

"How did I know what?"

"How did you know it was the daughter?"

"I didn't," Mayer admitted. "But there was no one left to guess, so I took a shot."

"It was a wise guess," the shaman said.

"I wonder . . ." Cassi paused. "I wonder how she became . . ."

"A skinwalker?" asked Mayer.

Cassi nodded.

Mayer shrugged. "Who knows. Maybe she killed her own father or maybe she killed the other witch. One thing's for sure, she learned the tricks of the trade from her stepmother."

Joe brought the drinks. Cassi took a sip, then pulled one of the ivory-tipped Marlboros from her purse and lit it. Mayer slid the ashtray over in front of her.

"Do you think she was really protecting the land?" Cassi asked, blowing out a puff of smoke.

"Vera or the skinwalker?" Mayer asked.

"Either."

It was something he had been pondering all evening. "Vera must have seen something in Germany that made her sympathetic to the Paiute's struggle to save their land," Mayer said. "I think she genuinely wanted to protect it."

"She had a funny way of going about it."

Mayer couldn't argue the point. He took a drink.

"And the skinwalker?" Cassi asked.

"She was once the daughter of a man fighting to protect his heritage," the shaman explained. "No matter what she turned into, there must have been some humanity left inside her somewhere. Just enough for her to want to carry on the work of her father, albeit in her own twisted way. Maybe she thought that as a skinwalker she could protect the land longer than she could otherwise. Maybe it took a while before the black magic overcame her soul."

"When do you think that happened?" Cassi asked.

"Probably when she took the lives of those twins," he said. "There's no coming back from something like that."

"The thing is," Mayer said. "If she was really there to protect the land, she would have had plans to kill Pierce and Hawthorne anyway. So why did she get in bed with Pierce?"

"Greed," the shaman said. "Simple greed. Why do something without reward when you can do the same thing for lucre?"

"Can you imagine what it must have been like?" asked Cassi. "For Hawthorne, I mean?"

Mayer didn't have to wonder, he'd lived it. He thought of Hawthorne in the trailer. How he would have been surprised, then confused. At what point, Mayer wondered, did fear overtake him? Or panic when he took the weapon from the drawer and fired it into the thing— the bullets having no effect whatsoever. He knew exactly what the man felt when he brought the gun, unwillingly, to his own head—just as Mayer had—only Hawthorne, unable to resist, was forced to pull the trigger. Did he know, Mayer wondered, that he'd been betrayed by his partner and made to play the rube by a woman whose motives were less than pristine? Mayer thought of the tortured face he saw on the coroner's slab.

"Did you take care of the ghost?" the shaman asked.

Mayer nodded. "I found the finger in an old vase and burned it in the fireplace."

"And Hawthorne?"

"He went up in flames along with it."

"Free to move on to the next world," the shaman said.

Mayer did not answer.

"How did the finger get there in the first place?" asked Cassi.

"The witch," Mayer said. "She wasn't just Vera Krupp's housekeeper. She worked for Hawthorne and Pierce as well."

"I don't understand," Cassi said. "Why would she put a piece of Hawthorne's body in Pierce's house? Wasn't she working for Pierce?"

"It's what they do," the shaman offered. "A skinwalker thrives on chaos and will seek any opportunity to sow disorder. The finger would ensure that Hawthorne's ghost would haunt Pierce. It was purposeful."

"She had the curse on Pierce all along, didn't she?" Mayer asked.

The shaman nodded. "Yes, once Pierce knew who she was, she would have had to kill him. She had no choice."

"It might have been better for him," Mayer said. His thoughts turned to Vera Krupp, her secretary Peg Westburg, and what they must have gone through when they discovered the skinwalker—the terror and confusion. If the shaman was correct, the skinwalker would have had to kill them as well to protect its identity. It would have been the perfect crime. Vera's crazed secretary kills her employer, then turns the gun on herself.

"There's still one thing I don't get," Cassi said. "Why did Pierce hire you in the first place if he knew all along he was responsible for Hawthorne's death?"

"The suicide note," Mayer said. "Pierce knew Hawthorne didn't commit suicide, but he was stuck with a crime scene that showed all indications of just that and a note that would likely stand up in any court. The skinwalker wasn't about to let Pierce destroy the note—probably why she just happened to show up that morning when he did—and Pierce couldn't let on in front of his hired man that he helped arrange his partner's journey to the big sleep.

"He felt his precious resort slip though his fingers, but then he came up with a plan. He knew the housekeeper had powers, supernatural powers—though likely he didn't know to what extent. He'd also heard of the Sloan Canyon incident, which meant he'd heard of me. So he approached the only man he knew who had been knee-deep in the other-worldly muck of Las Vegas."

"I get it," said Cassi. "He figured you'd put two and two together, which would lead you to the housekeeper."

"And Vera Krupp," Mayer added. "He wanted me to discover that she and Hawthorne were having a relationship. Knowing Vera wanted to protect that land, he hoped I'd find something to implicate her in Hawthorne's death. If he could get someone to prove the suicide was, instead, a murder, and that the supernatural was involved, then the note would be dismissed as false and he would get his resort back. I guess there was greed on both ends."

"And he figured you'd kill the witch," said Cassi.

Mayer nodded. "Or he'd kill her himself, which he foolishly tried. I guess he figured he could cover his tracks, or at least he was willing to take the chance."

"How could he possibly think he could do that?" Cassi asked.

"Easy. Rich people always think they're smarter than everyone else."

A motion at the bar caught Mayer's eye. Virginia had come in from the back and was now standing next to Joe. He motioned to Mayer and when Virginia looked over, their eyes met.

Mayer stood. "If you want to know what evil lurks in the hearts of men like Pierce, you'll have to ask The Shadow," Mayer said to Cassi. "Now if you'll excuse me, there's something I have to take care of." He downed the rest of his drink and was about to step away when Cassi asked him a question.

"You ever going to tell me what P. M. stands for?"

"You're a reporter," he said. "I'm sure you can figure it out." He took a step, then stopped. "Thanks for the help," he said to the shaman, and then to Cassi, "You're all right, kid."

By the time Mayer made it to the bar, Virginia had returned to the back room, so he followed. He pushed the door open slowly and stood in the frame. He wanted to go in further, but his feet wouldn't let him. Virginia was sitting in the chair at her desk. She turned to him, eyes heavy with the burden of having hurt someone she loved.

Mayer didn't say a word, he simply went to her. She stood and took him in her arms. Pressing tight, she said, "I love you, Prometheus. Please don't mistake my attempt to protect you as betrayal. If I thought there was something you could have done with those letters, I would have told you sooner. I promise."

Mayer wanted to be mad at her, but it didn't take. Instead, he wrapped his arms around the woman who'd willfully and thanklessly stepped in when he'd needed it most and held her tight. He stood there for quite some time—a boy in his surrogate mother's arms—enjoying the feeling of being safe, if only for a moment, and she let him.

"Are you going to be okay?" she asked, wiping her eyes.

"It's eggs in the coffee," Mayer admitted. "But I know what I need to do."

Virginia took Mayer's head in her hands and looked into his eyes. "Are you sure you're ready?"

"No," Mayer admitted. "But it needs to be done."

"Want company?"

Mayer shook his head. "No. This is something I need to do alone."

Virginia turned and took a bottle of Planter's Punch from a top shelf. "Here," she said. "You may need this."

Mayer forced a smile and took the rum. He kissed Virginia on the cheek then headed back to his apartment, waving to Joe with the bottle as he left. He stepped across the salt threshold and turned on the lights. He'd clean the salt in the morning—or maybe the day after. After draping his coat on the back of a chair and tossing his lid on the table, Mayer went to the kitchenette and found a relatively clean glass. He filled it with the rum Virginia gave him and set the bottle on the table.

One snort turned into a second, just for good measure. When the glass was empty, he filled it a third time and put the bottle down next to his mother's letters. All he'd ever had was her diary. The notes of a scientist, documenting clues and examining evidence, not heartfelt emotion from one friend to another. He ran the tips of his fingers across them—a voice from the past, waiting to be heard. Mayer wasn't sure he had the courage to listen, but he also wasn't sure he had the courage not to. He picked up the letters and examined the twine holding them tight.

He suddenly understood why the cigarette case had so much meaning to Pierce. It represented something to him—something powerful: the love he believed he shared with a woman. But it was a woman he could never have, so instead, he clung to the representation of that love. Even if neither the love, nor the case, were his to begin with.

Mayer took the letters to his bed, sat on the edge, and just stared at the addresses, both to and from, in her handwriting. Mayer had the worst handwriting possible—he left the tops of his a's open, and almost never dotted his i's. It was a constant source of frustration to his mother. And why wouldn't it be? By contrast, her handwriting was perfection. More like art than something utilitarian. The writing was perfectly straight, as if she held a ruler below her pen as she wrote. Her l's curved effortlessly, at the exact same height, slightly slanted forward. Her g's looked like g's and her j's, j's.

She tried to teach him, but it didn't take. He was far too busy with life to learn how to do something as useless as write properly.

A tear escaped down his cheek, followed by another. He downed the last of the rum, hoping it would steady his hands. It was now or never. He set down his glass, untied the twine, and opened one of the envelopes. After he removed the letter, he sat there holding it for the longest time—not able to unfold it. The rum hadn't worked. Finally, with a gut full of courage, he took a deep breath, carefully unfolded the letter, and began reading.

EPILOGUE

MEN BELIEVE THEY are so smart, that it is so easy for them to outthink a woman. She had encountered it many times, both in business and in marriage. Foolish boys. It had been an exceptionally long day and Vera was looking forward to a hot bath. She pulled off her boots and laid them by the bed in her secret room, then she went over to the tub and drew herself a bath. As the water warmed, she dumped in a capful of lavender-scented bathing liquid into the tub and watched as it foamed. Then she popped the cork on a bottle of St. Emilion Bordeaux and poured herself a glass.

After she set the glass and the bottle by the tub, she went into the closet where she removed her scarf and shirt, then took off her slacks and socks. She removed her bra and panties, then slipped into a sheer covering and a pair of fuzzy slippers.

She was about to turn for the bath when she stopped. At the back of the closet was a rack of long evening dresses that were not used as often anymore. Pushing the dresses aside, Vera reached for the dial on the wall safe. She turned it to the right, then the left, and then again to the right, before turning the handle and opening the heavy door. She reached inside and pulled out a piece of jewelry that had once caught her eye. A strange piece she had managed to sneak past her husband.

What she thought was a necklace, she now knew was an amulet—one with special powers. Thanks to Mr. Mayer. The Seal of the Seven Archangels. She traced the outline of the star with a finger. The thought of Mayer not wanting to search the room brought a smile. Men can be so easily manipulated. She placed the amulet back into the safe and secured the door, then headed for the tub.

She laid her covering over a chair, and placed her slippers at its clawed feet. Then she climbed into the warm, soothing waters. As she rested her head against the side, wine glass in hand, she decided it was time to learn just what that amulet could do.

ABOUT THE AUTOR

Paul W. Papa is a full-time writer and ghost writer who has lived in Las Vegas for more than thirty years. He developed a fascination with the area, and all its wonders, while working for nearly fifteen years at several Las Vegas casinos. In his role as a security officer, Paul was the person who actually shut and locked the doors of the Sands Hotel and Casino for the final time. He eventually became a hotel investigator for a major Strip casino, during which time he developed a love for writing stories about uncommon events.

Paul's crime noir book *Maximum Rossi* was a 2021 Best Book Awards finalist for Best Mystery and was a First Place Winner in the 2021 Next Generation Indie Book Awards in the same catagory. It also garnered a coveted 5-star rating from Indies Today. Paul's nonfiction book *Desert Dust; One Man's Passion to Uncover the True Story Behind an Iconic American Photograph* was also a 2021 Best Book Awards finalist in the catagories of American History and Cover Design and won the prestigious Will Rogers Medallion Award.

When not at his keyboard, Paul can be found talking to tourists on Fremont Street, investigating some old building, or sitting in a local diner hunting down his next story.

Maximum Rossi

Keep reading for a sneak preview of the first book in the Max Rossi Series. When a game of high-stakes poker turns into a boxing match, Massimo "Max" Rossi, the son of mob "fixer" Boston Rossi, winds up with more than he bargained for. All eyes turn to him when the police find his opponent, a hitman from Chicago, dead. And if that isn't bad enough, his only alibi--the dead man's girlfriend--is missing.

ONE

I WAS TWO eggs into a three-egg omelet when my breakfast was interrupted by a man who slid into my booth across the table from me. He wore a gray broadcloth sack suit, loose at the waist with narrow shoulders. His shirt was white and his collars button down. He sported a striped, straight-point tie and the wisp of a white handkerchief tucked into his top pocket. The man brought two goons with him. One was just shy of a mountain, the other a molehill.

His name was Salvatore Manella. His friends called him Sal. I didn't let that stop me. "Nice to see you again Sal," I said. "Please, join me." Sal was a New York mobster sent to Las Vegas to get a hold on things after the Siegel debacle of the 40s. He was a lemon of a man, sour as they came.

While the Molehill stood by his boss, the Mountain moved over to my side of the booth, blocking my exit, and, had we been outside, the sun as well. He wore a long suit that a family of three could fit under in a rainstorm. A Stetson hat, its brim curled in the back, sat precariously atop his voluminous head. He had a buzz cut high above his ears, a crooked nose, and a mouth to match. I took another bite of omelet.

"You're still here," Sal said, his puss fitting his demeanor.

I gave him a toothy grin. "Why yes I am," I said. "Thank you for noticing."

He leaned forward. "I thought we discussed you leaving?"

"No, you discussed my leaving. I don't recall being involved in the conversation."

I had come to Las Vegas several months ago from Boston for a friend's bachelor party and wedding. When it was all over and done, they left, I stayed behind. What can I say? The fat city enamored me. Blinking lights, free cocktails, great entertainment, oh yeah, and showgirls, lots of showgirls. I was hooked. There was nothing for me in Boston anyway, except, of course, the family business.

A waitress came and offered coffee. I moved my cup for her to top it off, but the Mountain sent her away.

"I'll ask you again," Sal said. "Why are you here?"

"I like the food."

It wasn't the answer Sal was looking for. It wasn't the answer the Mountain was looking for either. He reached in and placed a firm hand on my shoulder. "Mr. Manella asked you a question," he said. His New York-tainted speak was slow and steady. He squeezed just enough to get his point across. Had I been a watermelon, I would have burst.

I met his gaze. He did not look away.

"Tell Mr. Manella," I said to the Mountain, "it's a free country and, more to the point, an open town."

"Then you plan on starting business?" Sal asked. "Family business?"

I turned my attention back to my uninvited guest. "I don't have any plans," I admitted. "But if I did, you'd be the last to know."

The Mountain squeezed harder. I tried not to flinch.

"Want to call off your dog?" I asked.

Sal looked to the Mountain and nodded. I smiled. The Mountain released me but kept his hand close just in case.

"I'm sitting here out of respect to your father," Sal said. "But my respect goes only so far. Las Vegas might be an open town, but you know who owns it and it ain't Boston."

"From what I hear, it ain't New York either."

Sal smiled. "That what you hear? Maybe you should ask Lansky or Luciano."

"I'll get right on that, seeing how it went so well with Siegel." It was an unnecessary jab, but I took it anyway.

Sal grew solemn. "There's no room for you here Rossi," he said. "Why don't you just leave?"

"What, and miss the free buffet?"

"Always the wise guy," Sal said. "Maybe you should hit the clubs."

"I'll take that into consideration," I said. "We done here? I'd like to finish my breakfast in peace."

That made the Mountain tense up. I could feel his hand only inches from my face. If he could, he would've socked me one right in the jaw.

Sal dead-eyed me for quite some time, contemplating his options. I kept his gaze. Finally, I spoke. "If you're not going to leave, then make yourself useful and pass the sand."

Sal smiled. He took the sugar and emptied it into my cup until it spilled over the sides.

"Shit," I exclaimed, throwing up my napkin to create a dam for the liquid. Luckily the sugar was absorbing most of it.

Sal put the canister back down and slid out of the booth. He stood at the end of the table for a moment straightening his tie before he shot his cuffs, revealing links engraved with an "S" and an "M."

"If we have to have this conversation a third time," Sal said. "I may not be so pleasant. In fact, I might just send Vito here to do my talking for me."

I looked up at the Mountain. He grinned.

"Get out of town Rossi, before you get hurt." Sal said and walked away.

I looked at the mess in front of me and pushed the plate with what was left of my eggs across the table. My appetite had left with Sal.

DON'T MISS OUT!

To keep up with Mayer's adventures and all of Paul's books, sign up for his Noir Newsletter at:

https://paulwpapa.com

You can find out more about Paul

on his Facebook page at:

www.facebook.com/PaulWPapa/

If you enjoyed this book, please leave a review on Amazon, Barnes & Noble, Apple Books, Google Play, Kobo, or Goodreads.

Reviews help authors get noticed. If you do write a review, please let Paul know at paulwpapa@yahoo.com so he can show his graditude.

Books by Paul W. Papa

Fiction

Maximum Rossi

Rossi's Gamble

Rossi's Risk

Night Mayer

Non-Fiction

Desert Dust: One Man's Passion to Uncover the True Story Behind an Iconic American Photograph

Haunted Las Vegas: Famous Phantoms, Creepy Casinos, and Gambling Ghosts

Discovering Vintage Las Vegas: A Guide to the City's Timeless Shops, Restaurants, Casinos, & More